Sweet Mysteries of Life

By
Elaine Slater

PublishAmerica

Baltimore

First printing

ISBN: 1-4137-0962-1
PUBLISHED BY PUBLISHAMERICA, LLLP
www.publishamerica.com
Baltimore

Printed in the United States of America

Dedicated to Doctor Mac, aka Jimmy, who has always been there for me.

Acknowledgments

The vignettes in this collection comprise the experiences of many people to whom I am most grateful for sharing their stories with me.

Jimmy, Pauline, Kay, Elizabeth, Attila, Abby, Morry, Lisa, Howard, Mimi, Tina, Tim, Tam, Joanne and Richard.

I owe my most grateful thanks to Gail Noble, a busy editor who took the time to read the early manuscript of *Sweet Mysteries* and give praise and encouragement.

I owe thanks too to my family, all of whom have always provided encouragement and help.

Contents

Introduction

Throughout these pages, you will find ordinary people - even the few lowlife hustlers are ordinary. They are people you have passed in the supermarket, sat beside in the subway or bus, worked beside at the office. Some have been pushed to their limits by life or circumstance and fall over the edge and commit the unthinkable - or do they only fantasize about the unthinkable? The rest are like you and me - stressed out by the day-to-day pace, meeting life head-on, solving problems not by seeking revenge but with rueful laughter, perhaps finding in dreadful loss, hardship, loneliness or disappointments large and small, the confidence and strength that comes with moving on.

THE RUDE AWAKENING

She had been feeling warm, comfortable and loved when she was suddenly awakened and rudely pulled from a sound slumber. She had wanted to stay as she was forever, smiling through her dreams. Then suddenly her world was falling apart. What was happening? Her mind couldn't grasp it.

She felt herself being uncontrollably pulled, first one direction and then the other, unable to resist. The warmth that had surrounded her streamed away. She was cold and frightened. She tried to scream but could not. Was this a dream? What had she done to deserve such treatment? She had bothered no one, never shown any violence toward anyone - oh maybe an occasional kick or push to call attention to herself - but never anything serious, never with the intent to hurt. She had only wanted to stay as she was forever, never worried about where the next meal would come from or when it would come, sleeping most of her days.

But now rough hands were grabbing at her head. She tried to resist but had no strength. She felt a sudden gust of icy air, someone hit her and then a blanket was thrown over her. Why were they doing this? She opened her mouth to scream and heard, through her terror, only a weak wailing cry. As she screamed she gulped in a deep breath. The first breath of life.

THE WAY IT USED TO BE

The professor's voice droned on and on in a clipped British accent. A fly, buzzing above her, hit himself repeatedly against the ceiling as if searching blindly for something.

What was it? Something Marilyn had forgotten was haunting her. What could it be? It lay stubbornly encased in her unconscious refusing to stir. Why was it causing her so much anxiety? Damn.

"Miss Clayton," - her name startled her -"we have just discussed Macbeth's motivations in some detail. Would you care to expound on the motivations of Hamlet?" She got to her feet.

"Well…as I see it, Hamlet's motivations always canceled out. What I mean is, he wanted to kill his uncle because he hated him - that is, he was jealous of him. On the other hand, this violently powerful motive was canceled out by his equally violent love for his mother and his desire not to hurt her. It was a kind of…well, guilty love, I guess. Umm, so I would say that while Hamlet had very strong motivations which should have led him to direct action, instead of complementing each other, they nullified each other so that he was paralyzed."

"Very good. Miss Ellis, would you care to expand this theory for us?"

Marilyn was pleased with herself. She had really pulled that off and she hadn't half heard the question. But the persistent nagging of that lost thought marred her pleasure.

The bell rang. Class was over. Suddenly the shrill clanging released her hidden memories. When the alarm bell rang this morning, she arose, dressed quickly and got everything ready for breakfast. Dad was not down yet. She gulped her coffee and ran off to class. Oh yes. There is - was - something, but it was not enough to have bothered her this whole hour. There had been two places set at the table. She had noticed it without noticing it.

Oh well. It was really nothing after all!

She grabbed her books and dashed off to Psych. She loved this course, and she was a favorite of the teacher who called on her constantly for the right answers. This morning's discussion was about the relative effects of heredity and environment "Scientists have debated this point for years," Miss Hazard said. "It has engendered such controversy that unfortunately it has invaded the realms of sociology and even politics. Heredity or environmental traits, nature or nurture, are called upon to prove or disprove all sorts of diverse theories, but the fact is that we are still not at all sure of the exact part each plays in our ultimate make-up. Mr. Jessup, would you please give the class an example of a trait that you feel is purely hereditary?"

"I would say our appearance is purely hereditary."

"Mmm, yes, perhaps. But has not our appearance been refined, and in some cases drastically shaped, by environmental factors? Need I remind you of the giraffe?" The class laughed and Marilyn joined in." Miss Clayton, perhaps you can give us an example from your laboratory work that might indicate the effects of heredity or environment or both?"

This time Marilyn was fully ready.

"Yes. If you take a baby rat away from one of its parents - its mother, I mean - and separate it from her by a glass wall, you would see some of the effects. I mean, the rat, under normal conditions, might have been friendly and calm even while eating from the student's hand. But if you tear it from its mother, letting it see her but not reach her, it would become frustrated and its whole personality structure would change. It would snap at anyone who came near, possibly even stop eating. So you see, environment would have intensified and even distorted emotions that it had inherited but which might have remained latent all its life under normal circumstances."

"Have you conducted such an experiment, Miss Clayton?"

"No, but I've made similar ones and I feel positive that I am right."

"A scientist never feels positive about anything," Miss Hazard remarked kindly, "until she and others have made not one but possibly hundreds of experiments to substantiate a theory. However, your point is well taken, and I suggest you do a laboratory experiment such as you describe."

Marilyn was angry. *Of course she was right! And she had been in such a good mood when she left the house this morning. Why was it all being spoiled? She had slept well for the first time in ages, and everything had seemed wonderful. And now that thing about the table being set only for Dad and herself - why had it worried her? Everything was perfect. Dad was fine. She knew that because she had heard him come in late last night after the university deans' meeting. He had gone straight to the study where he slept when he didn't want to wake his young wife. Marilyn had heard him, but her stepmother hadn't.* The bell rang. Class was over.

It was too hot for field hockey, but that was what came next. So Marilyn headed for the locker room. She got into her gym things, cursing mildly when she missed her hockey stick. She dashed out onto the field late, incurring a black look from Miss Overbrook.

"Take your positions everybody."

"Uh...I don't have a stick, Miss Overbrook."

"No stick! Where is it? How can you play without a stick?"

"I guess I left it at home." *She was sweating now - it was much too hot for hockey anyway.*

"Home! Why would you take a heavy hockey stick home?"

"I don't know." Marilyn was truly puzzled.

"Well, we have no extras, so you might as well get dressed again and I shall have to mark you absent."

Marilyn was furious. *Why was this wonderful day turning out so badly? Oh, well, it was almost lunchtime. She'd get dressed and go home and have lunch with Dad. Just the two of them. The way it used to be.*

She ran all the way home.

HOW SHE REMEMBERS IT

Maybe it wasn't really this way, but this is how she remembers it.

A darkened Main Street, lit only by a few street lights which cast pitiful circles of yellow on the dirty crusted snow beneath. In between these disheartened sentinels, the street is dark and deserted. Flurries of snow blow scraps of old newspaper across the empty streets in the frozen silence. The red neon sign of the late-night cafe flashes on and off, while dispirited mannequins behind dusty windows, stare blankly into the darkness. Occasionally a car drives down Main Street and turns onto one of the unlit side streets. A woman, holding a small child tightly by the hand, materializes out of the shadows. She crosses to the bus stop, looking anxiously up and down the empty street as she does so. The child allows herself to be pulled along uncomplaining. The acrid cold cuts off all communication.

At the bus stop, one other figure stands, pinched and frozen. It is a young pregnant women. Her body is hunched against the wind as she scans the street for an oncoming bus. The year is 1945 and the place, a bleak midwestern town near which is set an air base. Perhaps residents will say that this is not how it was. Memory can be unreliable, but years later this was how she remembered it.

When the bus finally comes lumbering down the ice-rutted street, it is a lighted ark, its headlights blinding their night-accustomed eyes. The young girl steps aside so the mother and child can enter before she laboriously pulls herself up the high step. The warmth is welcoming. The three silent figures satagger to take a seat as the bus lurches from side to side, speeding off into the darkness with a rumble of gears .There are only a few others riding the bus - mostly young airmen returning to their base. Everyone seems glazed with fatigue, looking forward to . . . what? A military base? A rented basement room in someone's home?

The bus stops a few times in town to let people off. Several more silent people board, looking at their fellow passengers curiously, before settling into empty seats. Then the bus rushes on through the frigid night air, out into the countryside. The change is dramatic. One moment there are small dimly lit houses on either side of the road, and then suddenly the lights are gone and they are in a pitch black world. A sharp wind blows snow across the road obscuring vision. The driver fiddles with his headlights and peers through the windshield. The bus is a small cocoon of light, an island in a white void. Now, in every direction, lie endless fields blanketed in white. A few houses appear, seen through a veil of blowing snow. In their lighted windows one can sometimes catch a brief glimpse of life, of home, of family. The young pregnant woman feels an ache of loneliness that is almost unbearable.

Soon there is no one left in the bus except for a knot of soldiers seated in the back, heading for the air base. For a short while they are noisy, laughing and singing, perhaps for her benefit, but now as they travel along the deserted countryside, the mournful surroundings seem to envelope them too in memories of home, in silent prayers that they will live to marry, to see their children grown, to survive the war.

The young girl stares through the window into the night. There is no moon, but the snow's whiteness reflects the lights of the bus as they speed forward. She feels she is passing into a trance, hurtling through the night into nothingness. Twenty minutes out into the country, looking anxiously for a landmark in the black featureless landscape, the young girl pulls the stop cord. Glancing back, the driver watches her in his mirror as she lumbers forward. He calls out "Good night," as she lowers herself heavily onto the roadside. Before she has a chance to reply, the doors close. On each side of the road there are snow-covered fields stretching to the horizon. These are parted by a rutted country road which leads to a small cluster of houses.

The driver watches her for a moment in his rearview mirror as she crosses the road and disappears into the darkness. Then he lurches forward into the night. She looks back and feels a stab of fear. Everything frightens her these days. She is suffused with a sense of loss. And now the bus leaving seems to her another loss, a loss of warmth, a loss of community, a brief time when she didn't have to think but could just let herself speed into the night.

The wind howls across the prairie as she stumbles past small, lighted homes, their parlor windows revealing Christmas trees sparkling with colored lights and surrounded by festively wrapped gifts. Her sense of loss almost overwhelms her. She marvels that people still live normally in what has become for her a nightmare of loneliness and fear, cold and discomfort. A freezing wind whips around her legs. Frozen tears start in her eyes, but she brushes them away fiercely. She continues on her long walk to her basement room.

She fishes a key from her pocket. Her hands are frozen and she is barely able to fit the key in the lock. Her landlady has guests in the front parlor. She walks quietly past, hunched inside herself for warmth. They do not greet her. She doesn't look at them through the arched parlor entry but goes directly into the kitchen and down the back stairs to the basement. Her teeth are chattering and it takes a while for her body to adjust to the new environment. Even with her coat on, she is shivering as she gets to the bottom step. Set underground, with concrete floor and walls, the only light in the basement, day or night, comes from a lamp on the nightstand beside the old metal double bed and a single unadorned bulb hanging over a battered bridge table and two upright chairs which stand in the corner. This basement room resembles a prison cell. The air is always damp and cold. The cement walls suck up any stray warmth that creeps in. The landlady refuses to raise the heat because it becomes too warm upstairs, in her quarters. This is home.

Without turning on the light, she falls on the bed, tears streaming down her cheeks. She no longer tries to stop the heavy sobs which tear at her body. Finally her gasps subside - she feels a strange kind of relief as she lays wide-eyed in the dark room. She wonders if her sobs have hurt her unborn baby. She wonders if the baby cries when she does. She hears people upstairs laughing and talking, acting as though nothing terrible is happening in the world. They are saying good night and soon she hears the front door open and close, and then hears heavy footsteps going upstairs to the bedroom area of the house. She waits. When it is quiet, she creeps upstairs to the bathroom. Then she climbs downstairs again to wait. She waits.

Finally she hears a key at the door. She raises herself on one elbow as footsteps cross the upper hall and head down the back stairs. Her heart leaps.

"Honey?" The young man calls tentatively, not wanting to wake her if she is asleep.

"Yes," she says, and then, "you're home." Her greeting is freighted with contradictions - with happiness and sadness, with irony and relief. He turns on the lamp. He is young, so very young - only twenty. He wears the khaki uniform and bars of a second lieutenant in the Air Force. His hair is cut short in what is called a crew cut. He is small of stature, thin and compact. His thin features, strong nose, small mouth, reveal only a hint of the strength that lies hidden.

Coming from the clean cold air outside to this concrete basement, he smells the damp walls and the odor of damp wool.

"Why are you still in your coat?"

"I'm cold."

"Why not get into bed?" She stands up and they embrace. Her head falls on his shoulder and tears fall again but this time she quickly turns and wipes them away so he will not see. "How was your day?"

"My day-" she begins, but he quickly adds, "...and how is Mikey doing?" She smiles wanly and feels her swollen belly.

"I'm not very good to him. I have no appetite..."

"Did you have any dinner?"

"I went to the cafe in town."

"This weekend we can go to the base. They're having a special holiday meal." She nods. "God, this is a dump," he says as he climbs into bed beside her. "Have you found anything else?"

"There was an attic advertised in the paper today. I called but it will be gone by tomorrow if I don't go over there early. How can I get over there to see it and leave a down payment?"

"Give me the address. I'll drive over tomorrow morning on the way to the base. Does it sound any good?"

"How can you go at four-thirty in the morning?"

"If that's what it takes, that's what I'll do."

"It sounds better than this."

"Anything will be better than this."

"It has a closet and its own bathroom and it's high so we'll get heat and daylight."

"That's good enough for me. I'll take it sight unseen."

How far they both have come. The idea of a room in the attic of someone's house seems like heaven. They hold each other for warmth and comfort before falling into a sleep of disturbed dreams.

She dreams of her youth - a few short months back it seemed. There in the home of her parents, everything is warm and beautiful. She dreams of her college days, of courses and exams. She sees her father's favorite paintings, her mother's favorite books. She sees herself trudging through the frozen landscape to stand by the side of the road to catch the bus. She dreams of an icy wind sweeping from the North Pole. In her dreams, she sees the tail light of the bus she has just missed, and she is running after it and weeping. There will be no bus for another hour. She dreams of walking around the town before having her one meal in the shoddy cafe, and then, as an early winter darkness wraps itself around the town, she sees herself walking through the black crusted snow to the bus stop.

He dreams of college, of fall football games, of elm-shaded streets and the smell of burning leaves. He dreams of his widowed mother, of his father who died so young. He dreams of waking each morning at four o'clock to head to the base. He dreams of fear when the engines sputter. In his dreams he gazes at his maps and navigational instruments and cannot tell where he is in a featureless sky. He dreams of missions, of bombs falling and shrapnel flying. He dreams of life on a Pacific island, of quonset huts and rats and anti-aircraft fire.

Together, they dream of a plane falling in flames through the sky. They cry out in their sleep and hold one another. Far from their parents, their families, their home, their friends, they cling to one another, fiercely in love, afraid to look into the future. If they get the attic room, it will be home for a few more months. Then, his training finished, he will be sent into combat and she will return home to await the birth of her child, to wait for letters, for news, for his return.

This is how she remembers it.

THE WAY IT IS NOW

When they were first married right after graduation from college, he had never been able to spend enough time with her. They bought a cabin in Lake Country with no communication to the outside world, and spent every weekend there, walking hand in hand, sitting by a roaring fire, listening to the lonely call of the loons, lost in each other - that is when they weren't chopping wood or hauling water from the lake, huffing and laughing at the unaccustomed exercise.

But lately things had changed. Business commitments kept him occupied on Saturdays. He could no longer find the time to escape to the cabin. When she spoke to him, he was never quite there. His reading moved gradually from Margaret Lawrence and Robertson Davies to the *Financial Post* and endless market reports. He still sat through the arty movies - Fellini, Bergman - but when she tried to probe their murky depths he never contributed a word.

"Where are you?" she would ask in exasperation. "Am I talking to a stone?"

"I heard you," he would reply, jumping slightly as though she caught him at the cookie jar. "Your last words were precisely '...and the dog, of course, symbolizes the eternal evil in man.'"

She would sigh. He was listening evidently, but still...he wasn't all there. His mind was on other things, and all the newly acquired luxuries that his business success brought them could not compensate for the loss of her young, playful, loving husband. His sense of humor now seemed reserved for his business associates, who told her how he broke them up at the Board meetings. He worked long into the night several times a week and came home bone-weary. How could a man that tired exercise a sense of humor, or talk, or for that matter, make love?

They bought a house in Rosedale and hired a housekeeper. Now she had more time than ever to feel lonely. She scanned the magazine advertisements and decided that perhaps she was doing it all wrong. She bathed at twilight, donned an expensive pink dressing gown, made a mixer of ice-cold martinis and decided to eat by candlelight. When he arrived home, their favorite Mozart concerto was playing. He looked mildly surprised at her outfit, commented that she smelled good, said he preferred a bourbon on the rocks to a martini which gave him indigestion, suggested more lighting over dinner because he couldn't see what he was eating, picked up the latest *Barrons Report* and fell asleep on the sofa. His own snoring woke him up and he stumbled up to the bedroom.

If she had suspected another woman she would have had a better idea of how to fight back. But how does one fight an addiction to business? She bought self-help books and even furtively read *How to Get and Keep a Man*, a national best seller. Most of her friends now had jobs and she decided that perhaps she ought to be out in the marketplace working. She found a job editing a small literary magazine. But even that didn't fill the gaping void in her life. It kept her occupied during the day, but she still had to come home often to an empty house, or perhaps worse still, to a husband who never looked up from his papers or who stayed on the phone all evening talking to his business colleagues.

She thought about taking a lover, and had lunch with one of the young men with whom she worked. He showed an extraordinary interest in her husband's stock portfolio, and shuddering at the thought of a preoccupied lover, she decided she hated all men.

She began to brood. Her friends had children on whom they could vent their frustrations. She had no one. She mulled over the idea of suicide, but her other self kept calling out rebelliously,"Why should I die? I'm perfectly capable of laughter, of love! It is he who is dead already. It's not fair for you to kill me."

The *Malahat Review* slipped from her lap as she stared for a long time at her hands. When he came home that night she made no attempt to share with him the boring day's activities. He didn't seem to notice the deathly silence, although the housekeeper became so nervous that she broke a rare Minton plate. When the telephone rang just as they were having their coffee, he jumped up to answer it.

His suddenly animated voice rang through the dining room, "Harry! How did it go in Vancouver? I've thought of nothing else all evening..." She walked thoughtfully upstairs.

When he came into their bedroom, he was jubilant. He caught her around the waist and shouted, "The Pannoil deal is going through! Can you beat that? After two years of negotiating, it's finally going through. Bigness! That's the only thing that talks these days, and we're going to be BIG! I wish Harry were here right now, I've got to hear all the details. I'd..."

She interrupted him quietly. "Let's celebrate. Let's go to the cabin this weekend. We haven't been there in years. The road will soon be impassable and we won't be able to go again 'til spring."

"This weekend?" He looked dubious.

"Yes - we'll have a second honeymoon. We could find each other again."

"Have you lost me? Or have I lost you?" he asked in his old teasing voice. "Okay, honey, if you want a second honeymoon you'll have it. But I'll have to cancel two meetings on Saturday. How about putting it off for a week or two?"

"No," she said firmly.

He was too triumphant at the thought of the successful Vancouver deal to want to break the mood, so he did not argue. On Friday they drove up to the cabin.

It was just as they had left it. No one ever came near the place except for the field mice. There were signs of them everywhere in the house, but everything else seemed the same. There had already been a light premonitory sprinkling of snow in the area, but the woodpile and the ax were sheltered somewhat under the eaves. The wood was not too wet and they quickly made a smoky fire to warm the little room.

She bounced on the squeaky brass bed a few times and gazed about her happily. Far away, down at the lake, a loon called. As night fell, a cold bright quarter moon shone brilliantly through the pine trees. She set about cleaning and sweeping while he fiddled with his old short wave radio. Finally, flushed, tired and happy she collapsed into the old slip-covered easy chair by the fire. All the old warmth and affection began to return. Perhaps here they would find what they had lost. Perhaps here he would look at her again and not through her. Perhaps here he would be interested, if only for a weekend, in her, in her life, in her love - and forget the business world, which consumed him. Yes, she was ready to settle for just a weekend.

He sat opposite her by the fire, gazing into its crackling blue and orange flames. She did not light the kerosene lamp but the light from the fire brought his face into relief. The moon, shining through the windows, traced a pattern on the wood plank floor. She watched him tenderly, feeling the old love for that now tired, worn face. There was a distant, even a wistful look on his face. She settled back opposite him in the shabby old chair that they bought in a country junk shop when they were first married. They had loaded it together onto the pick-up that he had driven in those days, laughing hysterically as they struggled to hoist it onto the truck. The front seat was so loaded with their gear, that she had ridden the whole way to the cabin seated on that chair in the back of the truck amid a clutter of second-hand household goods.

How funny that had been! Everyone on the road had turned to look, laugh and wave. And when they arrived at the cabin after an unbelievably bumpy trip over miles of isolated dirt roads with low, overhanging branches that clawed at her face and battered the sides of the truck she had jumped into his waiting arms. Happily he had carried her to the threshold, where he discovered he had to drop her unceremoniously in order to get at the key that was hanging on a rusty nail. They had laughed together until they couldn't stand up. They had clung to each other for support. Yes, clung to each other.

She was deep in nostalgia. He lifted his head and gazed at her. She gazed back into his eyes, trying to guess his thoughts. Were they as far away as hers? Were they as full of love and the possibilities of love as hers were? He started to speak, and she leaned forward, a slight smile on her lips.

"You know," he began wistfully.

"What should I know?" she interposed softly and flirtatiously.

It had begun to snow outside and a rising wind was rattling the windowpanes, but inside everything was warm and cozy. The heat from the fire was making her drowsy and her lids were heavy as she smiled across at him.

"Central American Tobacco has just merged with Amalgamated Biscuit."

She buried the bloodstained ax in the snow and went back to sit by the fire - to lose herself in nostalgia again before she had to go look for the shovel.

A FUNNY THING HAPPENED ....

I musta been the last person to talk to him before the cops took him in. It's unbelievable. You never know what makes people do crazy things! You haven't heard what happened? I'll start at the beginning.

TGIF I always say. Thank God it's Friday! But last Friday was the worst. Just as I'm rushing out of the office, P. & S. calls to suggest a whole new promo scheme. How the hell are we going to manage that and still get in on deadline? My beeper shows a call from whats-his-name, the executive manager of Continental Supply. It's too late to return his call and I'm wondering what HE's calling me about. If it's another price rise, I'm going ballistic. On top of that, they're flashing the news on a giant TV screen that the market's taken another jolt. What a day. WHAT a day! All I need now, I'm thinking, is to hear that Sustenential Dynamics has underbid us on the new contract, and I'm through.

As usual Union Station's mobbed - crowds of commuters tearing around in all directions. The place smells of sweat, tobacco and cooking fat from the fast food joints. I'm thinking and worrying so hard that I don't even see where I'm going and I crack right into Al Newhouse. For a second I don't remember the guy's name. I'm not great with names, and he only joined the firm about six months ago. All I know is he's big and real quiet. Scuttlebutt had it around the office that his wife walks all over him, but she's a nice gal with a great sense of humor - usually at his expense. I met her at a couple of executive social functions.

Anyway, when his name comes to me, I give him a friendly punch on the shoulder and yelling so he can hear me above the noise I say, "Hi there, Al. I sure don't get to see you much. If I hadn't run across your name on an inter-office memo the other day, I wouldn't even know we were both working for the same great cause."

He laughs. I catch a glimpse of the big clock, and start to move.
"My God! I'm going to miss my train. Give my love to Evelyn."

"Evelyn?" he says. He sure is a sick-looking guy. "I didn't know you knew her."

"Sure do. Met her at a couple of parties. She's a great gal. All the guys get a kick out of her. Well, so long. I gotta make tracks."

I leave him standing there like a big statue with crowds swirling around him as if he's a permanent fixture. I don't know why the hell he's just standing there. He must have had a train to catch too. I don't remember where he lives. Somewhere in the suburbs.

Anyway, that was some day! First a zillion foul-ups at the office - this mysterious call from Continental, no word on Sustenential, a bear market, and then crashing into this poor guy. On top of that, the train catches fire and a woman has a heart attack on board and they have to call ahead for an ambulance at Oakwood, and I don't get home until 7:30. Amy is fit to be tied. Billy, Jr. has the flu and Andy is carrying on because he's got to have a shot tomorrow. Anyway, it's Home Sweet Home like always.

When things finally quiet down and Amy and I get a minute to talk, I tell her how I ran into Al Newhouse.

"Al Newhouse?" she says. "Oh yes. The new sales exec. How are Phyllis and the kids?"

"Phyllis?" says I dumbly.

"Yeah, Phyllis," she says.

"No wonder he looked at me so funny," I said. " I asked him how was...Elaine, Eileen, something like that."

"That's a great way to promote firm solidarity. What did he call ME?"

"He hardly said a word. Didn't correct me either. Too polite, I guess. I'll apologize tomorrow."

But tomorrow was Saturday, and by Monday to tell the truth, I'd forgotten already. But it didn't matter. Funny thing happened. Not funny really. Not funny at all, in fact. 'Cause by Monday it's too late to apologize. You won't believe why.

This big nothing kind of guy is in JAIL by Monday. You know

what for? You'll never guess. Murder!

Seems he was on his way home when I bumped into him. But then he changed his mind. Craziest thing I ever heard. Look - here it is, front page news too.

"SALES EXEC MURDERS MISTRESS- Alfred Newhouse, 42, sales executive with the multi-million dollar firm of Lucius Doddering Enterprises, has been arrested on the charge of having murdered Evelyn Kinkaid, 34. Ms. Kinkaid is said to have been his mistress. She was described by neighbors as a quiet, moderately attractive woman who almost never went out except in the company of Mr. Newhouse. Police say that Newhouse, who is married and has two children, has confessed to killing his mistress in a fit of jealous rage."

What do you think of that? And I actually knew the guy! What would make him do a thing like that?

THE HEADMASTER

Our son had just been accepted into St Crispin's School for Boys. My husband's late father had gone there on scholarship as had his uncle, so it was something of a tradition in his family. Nonetheless, it was a coup for Tod to have gotten in, as the school took only the best students from the so-called best families. I never have considered myself a genuine product of the latter, being of a rather tattered sort, more proud than ashamed of my lack of lineage, savoir-faire, and fashion sense.

I have always disliked social pretense or false courtesy so when my husband suggested that we invite the new Headmaster of St. Crispin's to dinner, I was more than a little alarmed. I had no experience in this type of social engagement and felt woefully out of my depth. Even the word "Headmaster" seemed foreign to me. At the high school that I attended we had a principal though she was formidable enough. Generally you only met her if you were about to be suspended for some infraction of the rules.

My husband, seeing my reluctance, assured me that he had met the Headmaster at his club and he was a nice enough sort, so I took a deep breath and sent out an invitation to Mr. and Mrs. Headmaster.

It was a rainy night when I answered the door to find, not the tall, grey-haired, distinguished looking gentleman I had expected to find escorting a tall, thin woman whose blond hair would be tied in a stern, but elegant, knot at the back of her neck. No. The couple standing before me was middle-aged, short and stout. He was rather bald and had a small mustache suspended under a long angular nose. His wife had a full head of dark permed hair tucked under a plastic covering, somewhat like a shower cap. She had only the slightest hint of a mustache erupting from the mottled area above her broad mouth.

They returned my greeting with some formality. Todd, then thirteen, watched as his mother took their coats and invited Mrs. Headmaster to follow her into the living room, the latter leaving a cloud of perfume in her wake. My husband greeted John and Myrna- "Please call us by our Christian names," they had urged us warmly - and offered them a drink. I didn't know if Headmasters and their spouses imbibed, but indeed they both accepted, indicating a preference for Jack Daniels. Then the difficult part began. We had to make conversation for an entire evening.

I am a bit shy under the best of circumstances and in this situation was counting heavily upon my husband to keep up a light yet learned patter as befitted the occasion. I felt tongue-tied and intimidated in the presence of this erudite couple. My nervousness dated back to the time I was sent to the principal's office for translating Caesar's last words, "Et tu Brute!" as "Oh, you brute!" My teacher had been singularly unamused.

Our son sat with us watching his parents handle his future. As soon as everyone was seated in the sun porch, and while I was desperately trying to think of something charming and witty to say, my husband leapt into the breach.

"Tell me, Headmas - John - where were you before you came to St Crispin's?"

"In Saskatoon," he replied, "at Drayton College."

My husband, bless his heart, turned to me and said, "Hon, doesn't your mother have a cousin in Saskatoon?" That was a wonderful opening to an amusing story that my sister and I had always relished.

"Yes," I said, delighted at the opportunity to say something amusing and a bit wild, "that's the cousin whose wife ran away with the Philosophy Professor." Too late it occurred to me that perhaps this wasn't as sophisticated a response as it had always seemed in the past. Perhaps John and Myrna, being themselves from Academia, wouldn't find it amusing.

I was so lost in my sudden panic at a possible faux pas, I heard only dimly through the mists, something shocking - a sentence that was not grammatically correct and emerging from the mouth of the Headmaster's wife.

"That was me!" Before I could grasp the meaning beyond the

syntax, she added, "and I hardly ran off with him."

I remember seeing my son's jaw drop. I remember babbling, "Oh, of course you didn't!" I remember that my husband, having led me down this primrose path, now stood mute, drink in hand, his genial smile vanished, replaced by something that I can only describe as a stupefied rictus of a smile. I remember thinking, *Surely there must be more than one Philosophy Professor who ran off with someone's wife in Saskatoon?* I remember thinking, *How can she be so convinced it is her - um, she?* I remember thinking, *How the hell should I have known that the headmaster had been a Philosophy Professor?*

The headmaster's wife, having said firmly that she did not run off with the Philosophy Professor, but who nonetheless had also said very clearly, "That was me!" would not let the matter drop.

"How are you related to Sam?" she asked. When I stared at her dumbly, having no idea who Sam was and hoping this was all just some terrible nightmare in which people said absurd things that had no relevance to the real world, she repeated, "How are you related to Sam, my former husband - your mother's cousin, did you say?"

How am I related to my mother's cousin? How am I related to the human species? I thought.

In my ignorance I had always imagined when my mother told us this story of her wild Western relative, that only tall young willowy things ran away with each other. People with names like Brock and Meredith. Be honest now, wouldn't you have thought the same? If this had been your family scandal, would it ever have occurred to you that your mother's cousin's wife, who had run off with someone like a character out of *The Great Gatsby*, was short, middle-aged and portly, and sporting a slight mustache to boot? Am I being terribly politically incorrect to say that it had never ever occurred to me that the man with whom she had run off was, in the modern vernacular, height-challenged, age-challenged and weight-challenged? Would you ever have imagined that two guests in your home, both of whom fit the above description, an august Headmaster and his wife, were the main actors in the theatrical drama that had scandalized your mother's family by running off with one another? I know what I am saying betrays a dismal form of prejudice. All of us, no matter our outward appearances have these terrible urges, and who can account for where they get directed, where they lead us? In fact, if short, portly people did not have these erotic propensities leading inevitably to further distribution of their genetic make-up, there would probably be no short, portly people left in this world. And that would be a great loss, I know that. After all, Einstein was not tall, thin and handsome with neat graying hair. Einstein was, at a certain point in his life, short, middle-aged and portly. If I remember correctly, he had a mustache too though I can't speak for his wife.

I felt as though I had become untethered from the mother ship and was floating in outer space."How is Sam related to you?" she had asked, and that question was still hovering in the air, waiting. I gave the only answer I could think of.

"Sam who?"

"Didn't you say he was your mother's cousin?"

"Didn't I say who was my mother's cousin?" I barked, unable even to bring a clear picture of my mother into focus. All I could see in my now fevered imagination, were these two unlikely people, their faces swollen with passion, their clothes disheveled, holding hands and running barefoot through the Memorial Chapel at Drayton, while gargoyles peered down at them in stern disapproval, and the eyes of the carved saints turned skyward in dismay.

"Sam! Didn't you say Sam was your mother's cousin? How is your mother related to him?" Her voice was brusque and impatient. She was dealing with some sort of idiot and she knew it. She didn't seem the slightest bit put out, simply bent on getting our family genealogy straight. As for me, I was clearly out of my depth. It was time for my husband to rescue me. He owed me at least that, having inadvertently hurled me to the lions. I threw him an appealing look, and he, with my halting help, began to trace my mother's relationship to Sam, my first cousin once removed whom I had never met.

The evening had not yet begun. We had not even gotten past our first drink. I wanted to run upstairs and drown myself in the toilet bowl. I wanted to black out and be rushed to some long-term care facility. I wanted to melt, like the Witched Witch of the North, into a little puddle of oil.

I prefer to skip over the rest of the evening. I have blacked out most of it in any case. I remember though that having finally closed the front door after saying good night to the Headmaster and his wife, my husband and I fell into each other's arms, overcome by hysterical, nay, maniacal laughter. It was all the more explosive at having been pent up during the long evening. At dinner I knew that if I caught my husband's eye, the bubbling drunken mirth would overcome me and once unbottled, would be impossible to re-cork. Therefore, although I sat opposite him at table, and although the conversation, as I remember it, ranged around such dreary and tragic subjects as Malthus and the famines that were engulfing Africa, I dared not look at my husband, but kept swiveling my head in an unnatural way, from the Headmaster who sat at my left, to his wife who sat at my right.

The following morning, I called my sister. "Alice," I said, "do you remember Mother's cousin in Saskatoon?"

"Of course," she replied, laughing. "That's the one whose wife ran away..."

"Stop!" I shouted. But it was too late for me.

Much later I learned from friends who used to live in Saskatoon that Mrs. Headmaster had indeed run away with Mr. Headmaster despite her ungrammatical protestation. She had signed up for a Philosophy extension course offered by Drayton College. Sam, who owned the premier dress shop in Saskatoon, didn't have the energy or perhaps the inclination, to join her. So she went alone to improve her mind, every Tuesday night. But it wasn't only her mind that improved. Her sex life seems to have improved as well.

Soon, it was noticed by the other students, most of whom were women and perhaps by reason of their gender more prone to notice such details, that Myrna was staying late ever more frequently to ask questions presumably about Manichaeism and the Schismatics, or perhaps to discuss translations of the writings of Zeno of Citium.

John was then still a bachelor. When he was younger (and still had his hair) he had been too deep into his writings to have been able to find a woman who shared his interests in Neo-Hegelian thought or his book on the philosophy of Albertus Magnus. And then suddenly he was bald and older and he gave up trying to find a helpmate.

Drayton College had strict rules about teachers fraternizing with students, although the boundaries of proper behavior became somewhat permeable when applied to extension courses and adult students. However, when the breach concerned a married woman and the wife of one of the city's best known and well-liked citizens, action was called for. Although he had tenure at the college, the professor was called in to face the Board. Shortly thereafter he presented his resignation, effective at the end of the year, and the affair was never mentioned again. That is until I brought it back, front and center.

"That was me, and I hardly ran away with him!" she had said.

The Headmaster and his wife only stayed at St. Crispin's for two years. My son left before they did. It turned out that Todd was not as happy as his father had been at the school. Early in the year, he had fumbled a pass during the Junior Varsity Homecoming game against the all-school champions and thereafter had been permanently dubbed "Thud" by his schoolmates. He was called by that name for the entire year. By April he was begging to come home.

After that night, nothing was ever quite the same for me again. What I had imagined to be a refreshing natural manner in myself, indicative of an honest, unpretentious sensibility, I saw now as an unforgivable lack of tact - not the mark of a quiet confidence but of a tasteless absence of sophistication. Where once I would gamely force myself to make small talk, now I remain mute, bordering on autistic. People, I am sure, have begun to wonder what my husband sees in me. Sometimes I wonder myself.

SPECIAL IDENTITY - A PLAYLET

SHE
Well, what did they say?

HE
They would try to locate my birth
mother and if she agrees to see me I
can contact her.

SHE
And you don't believe they'll locate
her or you don't believe she'll want
to see you. Right?

HE
I don't believe anything anymore.

SHE
Does it really matter so much?

HE
Yes it does. Sometimes I wonder
why.

SHE
A lot of people are perfectly happy
not knowing....

HE
I know that. I wish I was, but I'm
not. I need to know who I am.

SHE
Don't you know that already? I do. I
mean I know who you are.

HE
No - you know what I am, not who
I am.

SHE
Well, I'm not sure what the difference
is there, but I know you're a good man
with a lousy temper, size 8 1/2 shoes,
grey eyes, two wonderful adoptive parents.

HE
That's what I am.

SHE (sighs)
Who am I?

HE
You are Katherine Tarnow.

SHE
And who is that?

HE
Daughter of Loretta and Abe Tarnow,
sister of Joe and Edna Tarnow.

SHE
In other words it's the Tarnow, my father's
name, that tells me who I am?

HE
In a sense, yes. But it's more than that.
Through your parents you not only have
a history but you inherit a culture. You
can trace your family back to Russia.

SHE
It was Poland, I think, and my grandfather
was forced to flee from his home so I've
rejected that particular culture, thank you.

HE
Well at least you had a choice.

SHE
You have a choice too - to give up the search
and to say proudly, I am Adam. History starts
with me.

HE
Like Adam, eh?

SHE
Yes and I'll be Eve although not from
your rib if you don't mind.

HE
Ah. You want to frame your own birth
history?

SHE
Sure, why not? Let's pick our own parents.
Look (calls him to the window) see that
couple over there? I've just made them
your parents.

HE
She's much younger than he is. If that's my
father, I think he's having a fling.

SHE (exasperated)
All right but you know what I mean. As long
as you don't know who your parents are you're
in control. As soon as you know - well, you can
be disappointed. Your father could turn out to be
a right wing talk-show host and your mother a
country club socialite. I can see her now, with dyed
blond hair, darkening at the roots, piled high on her head.
She's wearing pointy toed shoes and she's
on her way to the club.

HE
She is not! She's probably an academic at
the U of T. (She claps, delighted). She has
dark hair like me and wears it short letting the
grey show through and my dad's a journalist.

SHE
There you go! Now you're in control. Your
parents can be anybody you want them to be.
They could be the first people to walk through that door.

(The doorbell rings.)

NIGHTMARE

One minute the sun was out, and the next it got all grey and dark. I saw lightning way far off in the direction we were going, but I couldn't hear any thunder yet. A wind came up from nowhere and all the leaves on the bushes and trees did a belly flop.

I looked at Mom, but she was driving perfectly calmly as if nothing was happening. She looked too young to be my mother and for a second I felt sorry for her, but then I hated her again.

She was taking me to this summer vacation camp, and I didn't want to go. Cripes, how I didn't want to go! She showed me this brochure and it had a picture of the Director and all the campers posed outside of their bunks with their counselors. The Director was a bald, beefy guy with a silver tooth, smiling something awful. The counselors were great big jerks in white ducks and open shirts. They all looked too damn proud of themselves.

But the kids! I tell you it was the kids who tipped me off. There they were, standing in front of the bunks with their shorts hanging down, their shirts out, their hair practically growing over their eyes. And I'm telling you there was a look of such dumb misery on their faces, it'd give anyone the shakes. One kid in particular - bunk 9, I think he was - was practically screaming a warning at me out of that picture."Stay away from here, kid!" he was saying. "This is hell." But my mom was determined that I got to go to camp. And when Mom makes up her mind....

I begged Dad. I said, "Just look at those faces in the brochure. You can tell it's a crummy place!"

My dad has a fierce temper, but still he's an easier mark than Mom. But this time all he said was,"Your mother and I have talked about this and you must trust us to do what we think is right for you."

He couldn't see those faces like I could, and I was ashamed to tell him the truth. I was scared. Cripes, I was scared!

I tried everything. First I tried persuasion. I argued with them all the time. I told them it was no good sending me there because I wouldn't stay. I told them they couldn't make me go if I didn't want to. Finally I got sent from the table so many times, I decided to go on a hunger strike. I had nothing to lose, I wasn't getting much to eat anyway. But that didn't last long.

Next I ran away. I didn't get far - my bike blew a tire. Then I tried to be as good as I knew how to be so they'd want me around all summer. I must admit that worked the best. I helped Mom with everything, and when Dad came home I helped him wash the car and mow the lawn. I never even mentioned camp, but I could tell as the time grew closer that they were beginning to look at each other and then at me. They thought I wasn't looking, but I sure was.

Then the whole idea blew. We had a bang-up fight about my fingernails of all things! I don't know what happened to me. I guess all that helping was getting on my nerves. Anyway, I started yelling and fighting and boy, two days later I was packed into the car with Mom and was headed for camp.

We'd just reached this rickety sign, "Happy Days Camp," when I heard the first thunder rumbling in the distance. The storm was coming fast. A few drops hit the windshield as we bumped down this long dirt road, and I thought, *My God! She's going to leave me here*, and suddenly I knew sure as shooting I was gonna die here. I was screaming inside but my mom was still perfectly calm concentrating on this lousy dirt road.

The Director was there waiting for us with one of the counselors. He grinned at me just like in the photograph, and I swear behind his fat face and sweaty glasses I could see a deaths-head. He took my hand to lead me over to the counselors but I grabbed it away. His hand was like ice even though the rest of him was all sweaty. I looked up at this big counselor and I almost dropped right there.

"This is Archie," the Director said, "counselor of bunk nine - your bunk."

I sidled up to that big jerk and I whispered, I think I whispered, "I'm gonna kickyou in the head."

Cripes! He only smiled down at me, a smile that said, "Anything you can do I can do better, and harder, and MORE."

Then there was this huge clap of thunder and the rain began to fall in buckets as we stood there on this weedy parking lot.

I began to shake all over. Like, I couldn't stop shaking. I was gonna die if I stayed here - I knew it. But nobody would believe me, most of all the people I loved best and the ones who were supposed to love me best and protect me.

I was shaking all over and had my eyes screwed shut. Then there was this sound like a bell screaming in my ears. I awoke shaking with cold. It was dark with just a thin edge of light coming over a distant frozen horizon. But the alarm clock was jangling insistently.

"Turn that damn thing off," my wife's voice said thickly. She was laying in the other bed in a stupor, her eyes closed, her mouth hanging open like a dead fish and her hair in these great big curlers.

I looked at her in sudden revulsion and my trembling stopped. My God! She looked like my mother in the dream. I pulled myself up and got out of bed, picked up my pillow and stood over my snoring wife.

When I was finished, she still looked like a dead fish only this time she really was. Dead, that is. Then I smashed the goddam alarm clock and climbed back into bed. This was one morning I wasn't going to appear at her beefy father's plant or take any more goddam orders from her lousy brother, Archie.

JOSH

"He's not mine!" she shouted. "He's not even yours! Why must I care about him?"

Mel stared at her and then replied evenly, "He's mine. He's mine as much or more than if he were my biological son." He glared at her as she stared defiantly back. "I don't know who you belong to."

He walked out the front door and was gone. She knew this time she had gone too far. She'd never had a kid of her own, and this one with his sullen expression and one word answers, was driving her crazy. She really couldn't see what there was to love. Maybe if she'd known him when he was a baby like Mel and his first wife had when they first adopted him... Mel's wife's name had been Kathy too only spelled with a K. She died of cancer when Josh was eight and Mel had cared for Josh for six years by himself before she and Mel had been introduced on a blind date. If she had bonded to him when he was a baby she'd have something to remember, but now all she had was this galoot of a teenager who didn't know how to talk or to be polite. How could Mel expect her to love him? That was asking too much!

Her angry defiance lasted just until she heard the car start. She ran outside but it was too late. As the tail lights of the Camaro turned the corner, she thought, *Me and my God-damn mouth!*

When Josh came home from school he was his usual uncommunicative self. As he brushed past her she said, "How was school?"

"Okay," he said without stopping.

"What'd you do today?"

"Nothing." He had reached his room.

Feeling desperate, she said, "How about an ice cream and then maybe some bowling?"

He stopped and replied in his surly tone, "No, thanks," but he stood in front of his door for a moment, surprised.

"Oh c'mon," she pleaded. "It'll be fun and I'll help you with your homework when we get home. I used to be good at math and..." He was standing still, looking at the floor. Why did she suddenly care so much? His sneakers were untied, his soiled tee shirt hung out of baggy wrinkled chinos and he had his Rangers cap on backwards as usual. She felt revulsion. He was watching her.

Then he said, "Okay." She didn't know whether to laugh or to cry.

"What's your flavor?" she asked as they stood at the ice cream counter. She was aware of an almost flirtatious note in her voice.

"Vanilla." Always those one word answers as though he got paid by the word.

"Have you ever tried Rocky Road? It's delicious. Try one."

"Okay," he said without affect. After a taste, he said, "It's good."

Two words. She felt she'd won a major victory. He sneezed without putting his hand over his mouth. He looked like he needed a handkerchief, but she bit her tongue and said nothing. She took her paper napkin and gently wiped his face where the ice cream had spilled. He didn't say anything, but when she finished he shrugged her away and walked outside. The ice cream had tasted of her youth and as the sun hit her face she thought, *It wasn't that long ago that I was a teenager*. She felt young and happy.

But at the bowling alley she was unsure of herself. She hadn't played in years and didn't want to look foolish. The alleys were crowded with kids and a few older men in jeans or work clothes. There were not many women at this hour. The place stank of sweat and tobacco, though there were "No Smoking" signs all around.

Looking about to be sure no one was watching, she hurled the ball down the alley. It went straight for a bit then turned and fell into the channel. A big goose egg. Josh didn't say anything. On his first throw he got a strike and looked pleased with himself. After a few bobbles, she got her arm back and soon she was getting her share of strikes. When a couple of his friends came in, Josh introduced her as "Cathy, my step mom." She liked that. It wasn't exactly "My mom," but it was close. He hadn't said, "My dad's wife."

She treated his friends to sodas, laughing and talking with them, enjoying their admiring glances, until looking at her watch, she said, "Oh m'gosh, it's six o'clock. Dad'll be getting home and wanting dinner."

"I thought you were the liberated kind," Josh said, his voice now not surly but teasing. "Dad can make his own dinner. He cooked before you came along." Then he scowled as if he'd said something wrong.

"He did?" Cathy didn't miss a beat. "Well he sure never told me that!" She began to laugh. He had talked to her! She wanted to kiss the bowling ball. She felt lighter than air.

When they got home, it was after dark and Mel wasn't back yet. Cathy felt icy fingers of anxiety tighten around her heart.

But she said lightly, "Looks like it's just you and me for dinner." She rustled up some hamburgers and Josh helped with the dishes. "Some girl's going to be lucky to get you," she said, ruffling his hair. She had never done that before and he blushed. *What a damn fool I've been*, she thought. *He's just a kid and I've been letting him get to me.* When they finished, she said, "How about watching the boob tube?"

"I can't," he said, "Sorry." He went upstairs.

She was watching a PBS special when she heard Mel's car in the driveway. She walked out to meet him, her heart pounding.

"Where were you?"

"Out," he said.

"I had that figured."

"I have something that I want to talk to you about."

She interrupted quickly, "Josh and I had a great afternoon. We went bowling with some of his friends. We missed you at dinner. Josh says you're a good cook. How come you never told me that?"

"You and Josh went bowling?" he said.

"Yeah. It was fun." She turned away so he wouldn't see the tears that had come into her eyes. "I've been thinking, maybe it would be a good idea for the three of us to plan a weekend somewhere. It would help us get to know each other better. Maybe we could go to Disneyland or someplace like that. Josh would get a big kick out of it and so would I. And maybe we could ask him if he wanted to bring a friend along, I like his friends..." She was talking as fast as she could so he wouldn't be able to tell her what he had to say. She didn't want to hear what he had to talk to her about.

He didn't reply right away and then gave the kind of abbreviated laugh that says, "Try to figure out a woman!" But he didn't mention again that he wanted to talk to her about something and she didn't remind him. He liked the idea of a trip but didn't think bringing a friend along was such a great idea if they were to get to know each other better. She agreed. She was ready to agree with him on anything, except...

Later that night as she was ready to go to bed, she knocked on Josh's door.

"Yeah?" he said gruffly. He was seated at his desk working on a math problem. The room was a wild mess as usual. She had screamed at him two days ago telling him to pick up his clothes, put the papers away, stack his tapes. He had replied that if she didn't like his room she could just damn well stay out. That would suit him fine, he had said. Now suddenly the mess seemed like a benign extension of the boy, not yet a man.

He didn't look at her. He was probably waiting for her to start screaming again. She leaned over his shoulder.

"You've got that wrong," she said pointing. "The ...."

"Oh, yeah. Thanks." He crossed out his mistake. "How come you still remember this stuff?" His voice held admiration and she glowed.

"I used to be good at math a hundred years ago," she said. "I hated my math teacher though 'cause he only called on the boys."

Josh scowled and said, "I'd be real glad if our math teacher just called on the girls!"

When she kissed him good-night she felt the stubble on his cheek. It shocked her. She was shocked too by a sudden overwhelming feeling of love for this scruffy motherless kid.

"Good-night," she said, shutting the door behind her. "Sleep well."

She knew it wasn't going to be sweetness and light from here on in. She knew he would get on her nerves again and she would get on his. But something had changed for both of them. They could begin again. She had been given a second chance. Looking up, she silently said, "Thank you," and went back into her room where Mel was waiting.

THE TIES THAT BIND

I plumped up the pillows and then wiped the table off again. The flowers looked a bit wilted so I carefully picked over them, throwing the dying blossoms out and rearranging the rest. I looked at myself in the mirror three times. The third time, I said to myself, "What the hell am I doing!" But I knew I was doing. It was what I always did - and always tried not to do - when my mother was coming over.

They say an apple doesn't fall far from the tree, but when I fell off the tree I must have been blown away by a hurricane. My mother is a nice enough woman, and really beautiful to look at. But she is super meticulous about everything, superficial things mean everything to her and she's a real snob. She never finished college; she isn't interested much in politics or even in reading unless it's the latest issue of *Vogue* or the book that everyone is talking about. She's really smart too so it's a shame.

I suppose I relate better to my dad, but he's not that much different except that he's warmer with me. I can have good times with him - if we steer clear of certain subjects as we have learned to do. He used to take me everywhere with him when I was a kid. He didn't come to the school play or to see me play field hockey or anything like that. My mom did those things. It was expected of her, I suppose.

Anyway, as soon as I was old enough, I went as far away as I could to university and then stayed away until recently when my job took me back to the city where my parents are living. I dread my mom's visits. Every time she comes over we have a fight. It's always about something silly - she'll criticize my clothes or my housekeeping or my choice of friends, and there will be a blow up. I have learned to dread her infrequent visits, which I feel she only makes so she can tell her friends what a marvelous job I have and what an adorable apartment, even though I'm sure she doesn't really think so. It gets back to me though that she says these things, and I can only shake my head and wonder.

Sometimes my dad comes with her but this time he wasn't coming. He wasn't feeling "up to snuff" she said on the phone when she told me of her planned visit. I interpreted that to mean that he was looking forward to a round of golf with his business companions that he didn't want to miss. My mother said she was just going to drop in for a little while as she was planning to meet friends "at the club" later that afternoon.

I suppose, like everything else, it must be partly my fault, this divide between my mom and me. I do things purposely to goad her sometimes. I mean, today - when I know she's coming, I'm wearing jeans and a man tailored shirt. And soiled sneakers. I could dress up but I feel that would be giving in to her. This is who I am! I think.

When the doorbell rang I jumped and then looked at the door in dread. *Grow up, Kay!* I said to myself. *You're not a kid anymore. Don't let her bulldoze you.*

My mother looked gorgeous. I have to say that. She is not young anymore, but her grey hair is always done in the latest fashion, her clothes are carefully chosen to be in good taste but not conspicuous, her shoes always look as though they just emerged from the box, no scuffs, no wear at the heel. She hugs me, pecks my cheek and then stands back to look at me. I hold my breath but she doesn't say anything. I dash into my minuscule kitchen to bring out the teapot and my best little cups. When I emerge from the kitchen, she is straightening my pictures.

"What are you doing, Mom?" I ask, though of course I know perfectly well what she is doing.

"Your pictures need straightening, dear."

"Please don't do that," I say, feeling very mean spirited, but nonetheless self-righteous. "I don't need my pictures straightened."

"But you do, dear. They are not straight."

"Mother," I say with exaggerated patience, "I would like, for once, to have a real conversation with you, and it's hardly possible when you're circling the room looking for crooked pictures to straighten."

"I am not circling the room, dear," she replies in an even tone of voice, much as one would use to a fractious child. "Put the tea things down. What pretty cups. What is it you would like to talk to me about?"

She seats herself on the sofa, and I pour the tea.

"I want to talk to you about our relationship," I say in my most clinical tone.

"Oh? Is there something amiss with our relationship?" she asks as she bites daintily on a tea biscuit. "Did you mean our relationship? Yours and mine? Surely there is nothing wrong with it, is there? I mean nothing that's not perfectly normal."

I am staring at her. How can she be so condescending? "Mother, you can't be so deliberately blind as to say that!"

"My eyesight is perfectly good, thank you very much. I repeat, I see nothing so terrible about our relationship. Between any mother and daughter, there are a few rocky patches."

"Do you call differing about everything a few rocky patches?"

"We don't differ on everything. I think you are wearing your hair very becomingly today."

"I'm not talking about hair, Mother." I can't believe this conversation, but at the same time something inside of me is saying, *Kay, where are you going with this? Your mother is sixty-six years old, do you really think she is going to change now?*

My mother sips her tea and continues, "If you are talking about politics, well yes, I do disagree with you. I care as much as you do about poor people, but it happens to be my considered opinion that our business leaders are quite correct in saying that the poor can best be served by lowered taxes."

"I'm not talking about politics either. We'll never agree on that as long as you parrot Daddy in everything he says."

"I do not parrot your father. I have my own opinions." At last she was becoming a little heated. Was this what I really wanted - to upset my mother?

"Name one."

"Don't be ridiculous. But I must say that I don't happen to like the way you dress. I think that blue jeans on someone your age and build are most unflattering."

That got to me, the "your build" part. But she was still talking. "Nor do I agree with you about Woman's Lib, if that's what you call it. I like it when a man opens a door for me and I don't see any harm in that. Of course I don't approve of harassment or anything like that, but I must say it's hard for me to believe that every time you've left a job it was because of some sort of harassment."

I told you my mother was smart. And she knows how to put in the knife and turn it a bit, even in her most cultivated voice. Note how she has already alluded to my "build" and the fact that I have changed jobs a few times. Perhaps she even thinks it's all right to harass a woman in unflattering blue jeans.

"Thanks for your ringing endorsement," I say sarcastically.

"I'm not sure I know what you mean by that, my dear," she says, smoothing her skirt, pressing her napkin to her lips before setting it down. "I think you are very intelligent, no one could say otherwise. But how you use your God given intelligence is another thing."

"Mother, just listen to yourself! You can't say a single nice thing about me, can you!"

"I have already told you, my dear, that I like the way you are wearing your hair."

"I give up!"

"I don't know why you say that."

"I say that because no matter how hard I try, I'll never be able to please you or to reach you," I was standing up now and almost shouting, "to know what you really think or really feel inside that lacquered shell. How do you feel, for instance, when Daddy tells you to keep quiet, that you don't know what you're talking about as he did the last time I was with you both?"

My mother was quiet for a while. I began to feel guilty and a little sorry for her, that perhaps I had gone too far, when she replied, "Well, he was quite right, wasn't he? I don't know much about Bosnia."

"You know as much as he does. You're allowed to have an opinion anyway."

"I never finished college."

"Because he wouldn't let you."

"Nonsense."

That really got me angry. "You told me yourself that he gave you an ultimatum. He told you that if you went back to school and spent your evenings studying, he would find someone else to spend his evenings with."

My mother looked pained. She looked drained as she said slowly, "That's true. He did say that."

"Didn't you resent it, for Christ's sake?"

"Don't swear, dear."

"Well, didn't you?" I was pushing but I needed to know. Who was this woman who had given birth to me? Was there a whole person in there somewhere? Surely I didn't just emerge full-blown, I must have inherited some genes for independence or freethinking.

My mother smiled, but there was irony in her voice as she said, "It showed how much he loved me."

I wanted to cry out "Bull shit!" But I knew that would offend her so much that the conversation would be over, so I merely said, "He loved you so much that he didn't want you to finish school?"

My mother lost her smile. She stood up and said, "Kay, what is the point of this? Do you want me to become dissatisfied with your father, to defy him, accuse him? Is that what you would do? Do you want us to get a divorce?"

That truly shocked me."A divorce! No…" I stammered, "but…"

"Do you think you know everything?"

"No, but I…."

Suddenly my mother was a tiger. I had never seen her like this before. "Let me finish. I'm talking! Do you really think you know everything? Do you know that I once left your father…"

"You left Daddy? When?" I said aghast.

"That's right, I left him. It was many years ago. There is a lot that you don't know, a lot that I never wanted to tell you."

"Why? Why didn't you ever tell me?"

My mother pursed her lips in disgust. "I don't believe you ever asked. I don't think you've ever really been interested in me. You speak to me only to argue or criticize." I was still too shocked to take in what she was saying.

"Why did you leave Daddy?" I asked.

"For a lot of reasons, some of which you have already named."

"But couldn't you just have argued with him, put your foot down or something, without leaving him?"

I was reverting back to being a child again, a child that didn't want to see the established order of her childhood disturbed, all her sage assumptions smashed.

"I tried that. Have you ever tried arguing with your father? It didn't work."

"How old was I then?"

"You were four years old and you and I went to Grandma's for the summer. Do you remember that summer?" I nodded miserably. I had missed Daddy, but not that much. Grandma was different from my mom, much less exacting, and the two of them had their arguments but they were always amiable. When I think about it now, Grandma and Daddy were very seldom together. I don't think they liked each other very much. Perhaps it had something to do with that summer. But Grandma had died not long after that long ago summer. Thinking back now, that must have been a very hard time for my mother.

"What were you going to do?"

"You will probably laugh at this, but I signed on to go back to college. I wanted to be an architect."

"What happened? You'd make a great architect. You have such great taste." I was still in a state of shock. My mother had wanted to be an architect. I knew she was artistic, but I never thought....

"I studied all summer and got some course credits. It may surprise you to know that I did very well. But then your grandmother got sick and had to be moved to a convalescent home. I couldn't keep up her house by myself. I had to decide what to do, what would be best for you. Your father was begging me - don't look so surprised - yes, he was begging me to come home."

"But you had some money, didn't you? You could have gone on..."

"I didn't want to deprive you of a father, of all the advantages you would have. I had money, but not that much. I would have had to find a job to keep you in private school. And you loved your father so much. You still do, if I'm not mistaken. He has always meant more to you than I have. I know that. And he has been a good father to you in his way."

"I don't love him more, Mom," I said. My heart was pounding so hard I thought I was going to have an attack of some kind. "I don't love him more! I just felt that he accepted me for what I am more than you do. That he..."

My mom gave a bitter little laugh as she replied, "That's easy for him. He accepts things in you that he would never accept in me. You're the apple of his eye. You and your father, always together, with me on the sidelines."

"I never knew you felt that way!"

My mother sat down heavily. Her face looked drawn. Lines had appeared around her mouth and her eyes seemed shrunken. "How else was I to feel?" She put her head in her hands. "I gave up my life to bring you back to him and then I had nothing. He settled right back in his own ways. He'd promised to change but he didn't. So I threw myself into the life you so despise - my friends, my charities, the Ladies League. All I wanted was to be accepted somewhere. You're wrong when you say I carry all the same opinions as your father. If you only knew! I say the same things as my friends - but maybe they're not my opinions at all. I don't want to think about them, to argue about them. I have to be accepted somewhere, you see."

She was looking up at me now with tears in her eyes.

"Your father patronizes me and you despise me. Oh well." She stood up again and started toward the door. "I've made my bed and I have to lie in it, I suppose. I'm too old to change now." She started to sob. Her hand was on the doorknob. Where was she going! She couldn't leave like that.

"Oh Mother...Mom. I'm so sorry. I didn't mean...I didn't know..." I tried to hug her but she pushed me off, straightening her spine as she stopped sobbing.

"That's all right, my dear. I'm all right now. I have to go. My face is a mess, and I must meet friends at the Colony." She reached into her purse and brought out a scented immaculate white hemmed handkerchief. "Do change that lipstick, dear, no one's wearing pink this season," she said, as she departed.

ESCAPE

Climbing onto the shabby bus, Elizabeta looked neither right nor left. The stale odor of cheap tobacco mixed with sweat and kitschy perfume hit her with the impact of a blow. She felt faintly ill. A few people were already seated in the hot airless bus, but most of her fellow travelers were milling about outside, saying last minute good-byes. No one had come to wish her good-bye. Indeed she had dared not tell anyone of her plans. Anyone except Anton, of course. If her mother had found out she would have reported Elizabeta to the authorities without compunction. Hadn't she said just yesterday, "If a child of mine ever tried something like that, I'd go running down to the police and turn him in"? Was that a warning? Did her mother suspect, or was it just part of her never-ending threats? Well, the die was cast.

Out of the corner of her eye, she caught sight of Anton. He was seated toward the back of the bus on the left side. They mustn't recognize one another - they had decided they must sit apart at least at the start of the trip. She had protested that they could pretend to greet each other, to introduce themselves as though they were strangers, and then sit beside one another. But he had said not to take any chances, not to sit beside him- that it would be best to ignore one another at the start. But now she was so unsettled, so unsure of what she was doing, she found herself stopping at his seat and reaching overhead to place her meager belongings on the rack.

"Not here!" he hissed. Startled, she dropped her purse and her magazines. Not daring to look at him, she turned away and seated herself across the aisle by the window. She was shaking. Almost at once, a voice beside her made her jump.

"Is this taken?" A large beefy man was pointing to the seat beside her. He was dressed in a creased striped shirt open at the neck. His trousers were baggy and hung low over his belly. He wore sandals and no socks. He smelled of sweat and schnapps. His voice was loud and disinterested. She shook her head.

"Please," she said. He sat down heavily, his fat arms pushing hers off the arm rest. He took a small bottle out of his back pocket and took a swig. *Oh God*, Elizabeta thought.

She shrank down into her torn leather seat and opened her magazine. His odor was unbearable. She stood up and fighting by his heavy legs stretched in front leaving no room for her to pass, she almost fell onto him as she rushed to get to the aisle. He made no move to stand or move out of her way, but just grunted, "What's your hurry, lady?"

Once outside, she breathed in the fresh air and then, seeing his heavy lidded eyes staring out at her, she quickly sought the small, filthy washroom in the bus station. When she returned, she saw that he had moved to the window seat, avoiding her eyes. She quickly seated herself next to an elderly woman near the front of the bus. Unable to concentrate on her magazine, she stared out the front window. The bus was due to leave at any moment and the last of the travelers were coming on board, hoisting their luggage onto the overhead racks and calling out loud farewells and last minute instructions.

"Is this your first trip out?" the woman beside her asked.

"Yes," she said.

"Are you traveling alone?"

"Yes."

"No husband, no children?"

"No."

"Not even a boyfriend, a pretty girl like you?"

"No." Why was she asking so many questions? What did she suspect? The woman, with her short cropped grey hair and shapeless floral cotton dress might be innocent enough, but one never knew.

On the other hand, not answering questions fully was a sure sign of a guilty conscience, so Elizabeta forced herself to turn to her and said with a cheeriness she did not feel, "May I introduce myself? I am Elizabeta Semel. It is my first trip abroad and I am feeling a little nervous. I begged my mother to come see me off, but she had to be at her office and she...."

Now she was talking too much. Oh God! But the woman didn't seem to notice and soon she was telling Elizabeta how after twenty years of working in the same stocking factory she had decided to apply for permission to take this trip. Her mother was supposed to have come with her but she had fallen and hurt her leg the day before their departure. Carlotta, that was her name, assured Elizabeta that she would never have left her mother, but her mother had insisted that she go, and their dear neighbor Ilse Harnik, promised to stop in every day and to get her mother whatever was needed.

And so she chatted on and Elizabeta was glad for the opportunity simply to sit back and listen to what seemed like an extraordinarily ordinary and uncomplicated life. She was only required to shake her head in agreement from time to time, or to interject, "Oh dear," at the appropriate times.

Beyond the confines of the bus, the landscape sped by. At first the sooty environs of the city, then as they got further away, the outlying dachas of the important politicians and government favorites gave way to tiny huts and peasant cottages. Cars on the roadway pulled over to pass horse drawn carts as the peasants brought their produce to provincial towns and returned with empty carts and full pockets.

The summer had been a hot one with not enough rain, and the crops looked parched and dusty. After a while, even Carlotta got tired of talking, and both women put their heads back and closed their eyes. The roadbed was pitted and the bus rattled and jounced over ruts and gullies. When they had been traveling for several hours, almost at the town of L , someone got up in the back of the bus and holding on as the bus rocked, throwing him from side to side, came forward to speak to the driver and the Tour Director. As he came abreast of Elizabeta the bus veered to pass a cyclist, and he was thrown against her, grabbing her shoulder to steady himself. She opened her eyes in fright and looked up at Anton. But his eyes said nothing.

"I'm so sorry Madame," he said. "The bus is very unsteady." She nodded. He continued on, talked for a moment with the Tour Leader, who was smiling and nodding, and then walked unsteadily back to his seat without looking right or left. After he was once again seated, the Tour Leader picked up his microphone and in a scratchy garbled voice announced that at the request of a few of the passengers, they would stop at L so people could get out and stretch their legs, have a soft drink and use the facilities.

The bus shuddered to a stop at a shabby restaurant. People trailed out. Elizabeta and her seat mate waited until everyone else had left and then they too climbed out. Some passengers had gone inside to buy food or use the facilities. Others stood outside smoking and talking. Anton walked up to Elizabeta. She looked at him fearfully.

"Sorry I bumped into you like that," he said. "I didn't mean to wake you. I guess we should all get all the sleep we can get. It's going to be a long ride to Milan." Elizabeta nodded. "May I introduce myself," he said casually. "My name is Anton Jumec."

"I am Elizabeta Semel," she replied as they shook hands formally.

"Why have you decided to take this trip?" he asked.

"Well, you see," they had carefully rehearsed this, "I am an artist and I..."

"You are an artist," he said loudly. Others turned to look at the couple. "I am too! How extraordinary. Where did you study?"

He knew very well where she had studied as it was in art school that they had met. They hadn't noticed each other at first, but then when they were paired on a huge mural on the wall of the school, a mural showing happy farmers and factory workers, they had gotten to know one another. She liked his wry sense of humor, his ironc remarks about the work on which they were engaged. He had liked her reserve, her frankness, her implicit understanding of where he was coming from.

But after art school they had gone their separate ways. Then three months ago they had met in the street. He had iinvited her to a cafe. His eyes were different. They had deep blackish rings under them.

"Are you ill?" she had asked.

"No," he had replied. "Just stressed, I guess."

"About what - may I ask."

"Perhaps some day I will tell you," he had replied, smiling sadly. And one day he did tell her. He was planning to flee. He felt he could trust her, he said. In fact, he invited her to come with him. He told her that he had an uncle in Canada, a man he hardly knew, but who would sponsor him he thought, if he could get out of Hungary. He and Elizabeta could get married and live in Canada, he said.

She had stared at him so long that he became frightened that she would turn him in. But then she nodded slowly. Yes, she wanted to go with him. She too wanted to leave Hungary and try to make another life somewhere. She had never thought about actually attempting such a flight, except as everyone dreamed of a better place, but now there was a chance and she wasn't going to let it go.

So they met "accidentally" in hidden spots where no one they knew would see them together, and plotted. Then they met no more for three months. Their applications to take this trip abroad were sent in on different dates. Each said they were traveling alone.

Now that chance meeting was what had brought Elizabeta to L on the Hungarian border. And she was making small talk with the man she had said she would marry. It seemed surreal.

When she climbed back on the bus, everyone had noticed their new friendship; her seat mate said, "I see you have a man friend now."

Elizabeta blushed and shrugged.

"He is very handsome. Why don't you ask if you can sit with him instead of with an old lady like me?" Elizabeta protested, but the woman waved her off. "Women have to be aggressive these days. "Perhaps you have a boyfriend at home?" Elizabeta shook her head.

"I have not time for that," she said. "I live with my mother..."

"Ah," her seat mate said, suddenly serious. "I know what that is. Don't get caught in that trap. Make a life for yourself. Your mother has had her life."

They settled into a comfortable silence as the bus rushed forward again. At the Hungarian border, unsmiling guards came aboard and studied each passport, opening their bags and sifting through their meager belongings. It took hours. The passengers stood outside, stamped their feet in the cool air, and smoked one cigarette after another. Finally they were under way again. At the Italian border, the customs people were casual and the process went very quickly. Night had fallen and it was too dark to see very much as they sped through dimly lit towns and villages. They opened paper bags and took out sandwiches; the bus was smoky, and Elizabeta closed her eyes and tried to sleep.

When the bus finally arrived in Milan they were taken past the railroad station to a small hotel nearby. Before they settled into their assigned rooms, the Tour Leader warned that no one should go off by themselves, that they would all meet for breakfast at 8:30 - there were groans - and then would begin a heavy day of sightseeing.

As they had planned, Elizabeta told her assigned roommate that she got up often during the night and hoped that she would not bother her opening and shutting the door. But her roommate assured her that she slept like a log - and fortunately she did.

In early morning hours, Elizabeta dressed in the darkness. Then, leaving her suitcase open on the rack, she took with her only a small knapsack containing one change of clothes and a few essentials. She could have been any tourist as she walked past the desk manager who barely looked up, as she walked out. The streets were just getting light and she panicked when looking first one way and then the other, along the deserted street, she saw no sign of Anton. Then suddenly he appeared from behind the corner. He beckoned to her and disappeared again. She hurried toward him thinking, *The die is cast. I have thrown in my lot now with this man that I hardly know. I have left my mother, my friends, my country, my language, my culture - everything. For what? Where am I going? Where is Canada? What will happen to us? To me?*

When she turned the corner, Anton took her hand. It was as cold as hers, and she realized that he too was frightened and perhaps having second thoughts. That frightened her even more. She wanted to start to run toward the station, but he held her back.

58

"Elizabeta," he said. "Wait. Are you sure you want to do this? There is still time to go back. No one knows we have left."

"What are you saying?" she panted, her breath coming in gasps. "Do you want to turn back?"

"I am asking you if you still want to go."

"You want me to make the decision? Me?"

"Yes."

"But why...you asked me to come, you...."

"I am the boat," he said, "but you are the wind that will fill the sails. I will not go unless you come with me."

What did this mean? That he was the solid and she was the abstract - the influence without power? Or did it mean that they would be equal partners in life, for a sail boat rocks adrift without a steadying wind.

This time Elizabeta did not hesitate. "Let's not stand here. Let's get to the station!" she said and still holding hands, they began to run, and as they ran they saw people beginning to emerge from their homes. At first there were just a few early morning pedestrians. As more people joined them, headed for work, they felt too conspicuous running and they slowed down to a walk.

At the large station, they found the ticketmaster. It was their plan to take the first train to Rome and ask asylum at the Canadian Embassy there. Italy did not want refugees crowding their shores, so anyone found without proper papers by the Italian police, would be shipped back to their country of origin. That meant certain imprisonment. But they looked like anyone else. If they didn't speak, they could be taken for Italians, or ordinary tourists.

At the border they had had an opportunity to change their Hungarian dinars into lira. And now Anton shoved some money at the ticketmaster, saying, "Roma" and holding up two fingers to indicate that there were two of them traveling. The ticketmaster looked at them shrewdly, then counted out the money, shoving some back to Anton as he handed him the tickets. In the station, they felt exposed. The train would not come until 8:27, just about the time when the group was to meet in the hotel dining room. But their roommates might miss them before that and raise the alarm. They found a small smoky cafe nearby and ordered a roll and coffee as they watched and waited. The cafe afforded them a good vantage point from which to watch the street.

It seemed a very long time, but soon they saw well dressed businessmen with briefcases and hats, and fashionable looking women with husbands and children, heading into the station, hurrying to catch the morning train to Rome. They left some money on the table and walked back warily.

Elizabeta did not allow herself to relax until the train had finally gotten underway. It stayed huffing and steaming in the station for what seemed an endless amount of time, with uniformed police all around. Only when the train finally began to pick up speed did a great load fell away from them and Elizabeta allowed herself to marvel at the fashionable women, the beautiful buildings, the lush landscape. She felt excited and happy and she turned to smile at Anton who smiled back. Maybe they would really make it. Maybe it would really happen. Then she remembered what she had given up back home, and wondered if Anton would always love her. What if his uncle didn't like her? What if...What if.... Her smile faded.

In Rome, they studied their map and tried in vain to find the Canadian Embassy on it. Finally, they decided to walk into a hotel and ask in their few words of broken English. It was taking a chance. They decided that they would not go in together - just one of them - Elizabeta thought a woman would be best, although her English was not as good as Anton's and neither of them was fluent. The hotel concierge scarcely looked up when Elizabeta approached him. He shook his head when she asked for the Canadian Embassy, located a book of some kind, turned its pages and finally saying, "Ah..." he wrote out the address on a piece of paper for her.

"Is far?" she inquired.

He scowled and nodded. "Very far. Is best you take taxi. I get you one." Before she could remonstrate — their funds were getting low — he motioned to the man at the door who led her to a taxi waiting outside. She motioned to Anton and soon they were riding through the streets of Rome, wondering if their money would last.

The streets were filled with chattering people. How Elizabeta envied their seeming nonchalance, their absence of fear, their ability to be concerned only about life's little everyday problems. Everything was so different from the grey atmosphere of her city. Even the quality of light was different.

The taxi deposited them outside the Canadian Embassy, a grand and imposing building, in a very lovely area of similar buildings. Elizabeta left Anton to figure out what they owed the taxi driver, as she walked up to the front gates. They were minutes away from safety, she thought. Anton was coming to join her. A man stood by the front door. When he saw her approaching, he said in English, "Is closed today." She looked so dismayed and startled, that he added, "Is Canadian holiday. Come back tomorrow."

Elizabeta fought down the panic that created a roaring in her ears and forced herself to smile. She turned to Anton and said in her broken English, "We come again tomorrow to visit our friend. Is closed today." Anton just stood there staring at her. She had to say something so the man wouldn't be suspicious. But what?

"Come," she said, forcing a laugh, "now we go home and I make you wonderful meal for holiday!" She took his arm and they walked away from the Embassy.

What would they do now? They didn't have money for a hotel, but in any case, they could not have registered at a hotel as their passports were in the hands of the tour guide. They would have to spend the night in the street and how could they do that without being picked up by the police? So near. They were so near. If they were picked up by the Italian police it meant forced return to Hungary, imprisonment, their lives ruined, their artistic dreams smashed. Elizabeta felt the man watching as they left. They both were sure they felt his eyes on their backs.

Time is an uncertain friend. When you want it to run swiftly, it moves with manacled feet. When you want it to hold back, it flees as though in terror.

For Elizabeta and Anton, time did not prove friendly. The hours seemed loathe to move as Elizabtha and Anton walked around the city as if in a daze. Finally, exhausted, they sank onto a bench in a small park and pretended to be studying the pigeons and the many mangy looking cats that slunk through the park. They envied the people who looked so carefree as they moved quickly from one place to another, or strolled arm in arm through the park. They watched groups of nuns, huddled together in their stiff white caps and black robes like a group of penguins. They saw tonsured monks in loose brown robes, and gaggles of children emerging from school full of animal spirits. When evening finally drew near, they ventured to take a small meal at a cafe near a movie theatre. They entered the movie theatre in time for the last show. They didn't understand a word, but the flickering images on the screen kept their thoughts away from the fearsome present. When the theatre emptied out, it wasn't yet midnight. The Embassy would not open until nine in the morning.

They walked and walked, avoiding the police who strolled nonchalantly about the city. Finally, when they could walk no more, they found the park bench again and leaning against one another they tried to sleep. But they were too frightened that a policeman might find them and ask to see their papers, so they spent most of the night pretending to be lovers who dared not return home. The night air had grown chill so it was not hard to hold each other tightly for warmth. And they were indeed lovers who dared not return home. The night had a thousand hours.

As it began to grow light, they darted into a cafe when they saw the proprietor lifting the heavy metal shutters. He eyed them curiously. They looked exhausted and bedraggled. But he shrugged and went into the kitchen to get them some coffee while they used the little bathroom to clean up. Anton shaved and Elizabeta straightened out her clothes and put on a little make-up. When they emerged they looked and felt more presentable. It was still three hours until the Embassy would open, but as they sat and nibbled on a roll and cheese, and slowly sipped their coffee, they felt a glimmer of hope return. Maybe they would make it after all. And strangely, for both of them, with the return of hope, came the return of - was it fear? Fear of the unknown. Fear of what lay ahead. Suddenly things at home did not seem so bad. Why had they been so precipitous? Now there was no return.

It was not long before the cafe filled up with early morning workers who smoked and talked and laughed and Elizabeta and Anton felt once more a part of the life of the city. Was this what freedom was like? Never having to worry about the police? Never having to be careful of what you said and to whom you said it? These rough looking men seemed so ...unafraid.

When they felt they could no longer stay seated at the table sipping long cold coffee without exciting notice, they paid their bill with their last few lire, and went outside. As the sun rose, the air got warmer and by eight o'clock, it was hot. They took off their thin jackets and headed back toward the Embassy. They wanted to stay close, but not so close as to be conspicuous. As they circled the block once, and then veered off Elizabeta thought she saw, could it be Carlotta? Was she too trying to escape to a new life far from her mother? Elizabeta wanted to run to her, but fear stopped her. What if it was Carlotta and she was a spy, sent ahead to catch them before they reached the Embassy? Whenever a policeman or a police car went by, a siren blaring, they looked up at one another and smiled and pretended to be talking animatedly. They looked at their watches every two minutes, each minute an eternity. At four minutes to nine, they circled slowly back toward the Embassy, arriving at the gates just as the doors opened.

END OF A PERFECT EVENING

The evening started out so well. They rarely got out alone these days. They usually took the kids everywhere, partly because they didn't like to leave them and partly because it was so hard to find a dependable babysitter. But this evening Jodie was on a school trip and Marnie was invited to a pajama party at her best friend's.

The restaurant was one of those new Italian trattorias, all bright lights, lots of color and hard edges with delicious smells coming from the kitchen. Huge pepper grinders and a round of cheese and basket of bread sat on each table. They ordered Chianti and listened to the buzz of voices around them. Stephi felt happy. She felt romantic.

Roger ordered minestrone and veal parmigian. Steph ordered Caesar salad and a wild mushroom risotto. The wine came and she took a sip. It tasted warm, woody and delicious. She felt a glow. It had been so long since they were out together. They had to do it more often. She held her glass up to the light, felt its heft, admired its thin stem and the way the light shone through the clear red liquid. She'd buy glasses like this one day.

Steph told Roger about her friend Susie who had a new line of belts and whose husband, Mike, was working on a web site for her. Roger told Steph that his boss was going to be away for ten days and was leaving Roger in charge. He told a joke he'd heard at the office. They laughed. Suddenly their conversation was interrupted by a loud altercation at the next table.

"If you wanted to go there why didn't you say so?" a man said angrily. He was heavy set, with thinning hair and full lips. He seemed to be about 50, nattily dressed. His face seemed to be in a permanent scowl. The woman was substantially younger, thin with short cropped dark hair and large eyes carefully made up. Steph noticed that her mini skirt moved up to her thighs when she was seated. Roger noticed too.

"I never got a chance," the woman replied angrily.

They seemed to have finished their meal. The young woman got up and went to the ladies room. Her companion sat sullenly turning and turning the diamond ring on his pinky finger. When she returned they walked out without a word.

Roger said, "He had no excuse for being so sour. With that young babe on his arm, he should have been walking on air."

Steph replied, "Is that all it takes?"

"Well, it helps," he said, laughing.

"I think it's you who should be walking on air, not him."

Roger rolled his eyes upward as if to say, "Are you crazy?"

Stephi felt anger but she said quietly, "Is that how you feel?"

"How?" in mock surprise.

"The way your expression indicated." She felt the fun draining out of her.

"What expression?" Roger asked cheerily. He was enjoying this kidding around.

Stephi rolled her eyes, repeating his expression.

"That's how I looked?" he said

"Um hunh," Stephi said

"All right. I'll try another. How about this one?" Roger crossed his eyes.

"I don't see that that one is too much different." Stephi felt weary and terribly sad. What happened? Whatever it was it had happened so suddenly. One moment they were having a good time, chatting and laughing and the next...

But Roger seemed oblivious of the change. "You don't like that one either?" he asked. In point of fact, by this time he knew well what was happening but felt powerless to stop it. He didn't feel like apologizing for such an innocuous remark. Maybe he could kid Steph out of it.

Steph said very quietly, "Not very much. Maybe you should try once more." Here was one last chance to tell her he loved her and was just kidding and he was lucky to have her and knew it.

But Roger was feeling perverse. He made a simperingly loving face and said, "Okay. Here's another."

"No." Stephi had stopped eating. The risotto had turned to sawdust in her mouth. She wanted to go home. She wanted to hug Jodie and Marnie.

"What d'ya mean no? What's wrong with that one?"

"I don't really have to tell you." She still spoke quietly and semi-humorously, but this was beginning to take a toll. She so desperately wanted to hold on to the evening but it was irrevocably slipping away and she had no control. He was calling the shots and calling them badly.

"You're hard to please."

"Am I? Why don't you try one last time. After this I'll give up." Last chance saloon. She looked into his eyes. Roger made another simpering face. He felt immediately sorry. He knew he had blown it but it was too late and he was too proud to try to make amends. She was just being silly anyway. She knew he didn't mean it.

"Well, I guess that's it," Stephi said, becoming ominously quiet.

Finally she had reached him and Roger felt immediately contrite. What a horse's ass he was. Why didn't he just tell her he loved her? He reached out to put his hand over hers on the little restaurant table.

"C'mon, I don't have to tell you how I feel. You know I love you. You know how I feel. Why make a big deal of this?"

"Why do you try to hurt me?"

"Come on! I didn't try to hurt you!" Roger said strongly.

"What were you doing then?"

"It was just teasing."

"To what end?" He pursed his lips. There was now a silence at the table and although no voices were raised, the magic of the evening was over and both knew it. The mood of intimacy and sharing of ideas, or just complete comfort with one another during which the conversation jumped from one subject to another, from the inconsequential to the serious, had evaporated. She motioned to the waiter to take away her plate, still half full.

They drove home in silence through the darkened streets. Steph asked herself, *Have I a right to feel this way? Was I simply fishing for a compliment? And even if I was, why not give it to me?*

He was thinking, *All I did was kid around a little. If she doesn't know I love her by this time there's no way to tell her. I work my butt off for this family, so I make a joke about some attractive babe and Steph makes a big deal over it. It's all about nothing. Absolutely nothing!*

When they got home, Roger hugged Stephi and kissed her. She returned his hug but did not kiss him. The hurt, the sense of missed opportunity was still there. Affronted by her lack of response to his implied apology, Roger got into bed turning away from her. She took longer to get ready for bed. Under the bright lights of the bathroom, she stared at herself in the mirror. She was no longer a "babe." She didn't wear skirts that rose above the thigh when she sat down. She shed a few tears, wiped them away, turned out the lights and climbed into bed. He turned back toward her and reached for her hand. She kissed his forehead.

"I'm sorry," he said.

"I know," she said sadly.

"Do you know what we were arguing about? I don't."

"I know," she said again.

FAMILY FEUD

My dog spat blood this morning. I got so frightened. I wonder how people in the Middle East and other places where there is never-ending war, can bear to see the wounded. I didn't mean to talk about Harry, my dog. I meant to talk about family. When I think about my family, the Middle East comparison comes to mind again. Family feuds. People who grow up together and love one another, suddenly turning on one another.

That's what happened with my younger brother and me. I always took care of him when we were young. As I grew older, I baked him cookies and sent them to him at boarding school when our parents were away in the Army. When we all grew up, he and my husband were in business with my father. Everyone seemed to get along just fine. My brother was handsome, funny and smart. I was always proud of him when I introduced him to my friends - as I always did. In those days, no one knew me without also knowing my parents, my sister and my brother, we were that close. My brother was also sloppy, often petty, unable to take any kind of criticism and a womanizer, but people didn't see that side of him so often. I liked the one side of him but not the other. It's always hard to separate the good from the bad in people you love, especially family.

He had a tough time with wives of course. Or, rather, they had a tough time with him. After two or three unsuccessful marriages, he settled on a woman who had been a model. She was attractive and efficient but very hard on his young children. He had custody so the daily care fell to the third or was it the fourth, and so far, final wife.

The feud started without my even knowing. We were older. My father began to slow down and to show small memory lapses. My husband wanted a change. We moved to another city where he took over and expanded another branch of the company. My brother gained weight, his hair grew prematurely white and he developed heart problems. Our dear mother died.

I worried about my father. When I went to visit him he would sit holding my hand and tell me how sick my brother was. My brother didn't seem sick. He had had an implant and everything seemed under control. I wasn't sure why my father told me this. Later, my father's second wife who had been his secretary, entered our lives. Some time around then, my brother stopped talking to me. I didn't notice at first. Living in different cities we didn't have much chance for contact and if I called, I would speak to his wife and not notice. She was calling us all the time then, telling us that my brother, her husband, should be slowing down, that we should buy him out.

We broached the subject to my father, but he wouldn't hear of it, suddenly turning on me in fury as though I had betrayed him. My husband watched with foreboding as my brother and my now-failing father ran the parent company ever downward. My father would brook no criticism of his son.

Finally things got so bad, that my father swallowed his pride and came to my husband to ask that he buy out him and my brother. It was only then that I realized that my brother had not only stopped talking to me, but he was telling mutual friends untrue, hurtful stories, urging them to cut us off, threatening that if they remained our friends they would no longer be his. Outraged friends called to tell us this.

How can I explain what I felt then? Shame, I guess, is what it was. Not because I thought friends might believe what he said. But shame that our family had suddenly become like so many others. We had been so close, so "one." How could this have happened? I pictured us all at the dinner table, my parents, my sister, my brother and me, laughing, talking, caring about one another, proud of one another.

I don't know what part my father's second wife was playing in all this. I want to believe that if my mother had been alive she wouldn't have allowed the family to break up. That she would not have allowed my father to take sides with my brother as he did. She rarely stood up to my father, who was an overpowering force to all of us, but when she did, on those very rare occasions, he would laugh and give way. Maybe this would have been one of those rare occasions. I like to think so. I know that when she was alive she and my father had a standing good-natured disagreement about how they would divide up their estate - always to their three children, of course - but my mother felt that what there was should be divided equally while my father felt that the neediest of the children should have more. I tended to side with my father, feeling that if my brother or sister needed help more than I did, they should get it. My mother didn't agree, always wanting to treat us equally even if life did not. She was a wonderful, gentle, wise woman, my mother. I weep for her even now, fifteen years after her death.

When my father died, he left everything to his second wife and her children and to my brother and my brother's children. Nothing to my sister or me. Nothing to our children, his grandchildren who had adored him. I didn't care about the money. I didn't need it. I cared about what it meant. What had happened to the love we shared? I pictured his cool, clean hands, his silken hair, the bear hugs he and our mother gave us when they returned from a vacation. I pictured how when I was little, he and my mother would come into my room after a night out to kiss me good night. If the sweet perfume and the rustle of my mother's dress or the scratchy feel of my father's cheek happened to wake me up, they would sit on the bed and tell me about their evening. How I loved them!

My father loved me too. When I played varsity hockey in high school, and captained the team, he came to watch the games - the only father there - praising me to others, describing how I had encouraged fellow team members or how hard I played.

At my father's suggestion, we bought the family business. It was very hard. We had to borrow a great deal of money and give personal guarantees at a time of high interest rates, falling business and skittish banks. But there was no other way. In the buy-out, my brother insisted on ten years of full salary and medical coverage. He tried to get a car and chauffeur too. The business could barely stand and he was milking it further. There were times during the negotiations when his demands made my husband throw up his hands, but our lawyer and friend, stayed the course and finally got a deal signed. My brother told everyone who would listen that we "stole" the business from him. We didn't know then if the business could be saved or if it would take us down with it. My father, now fully retired, also had his salary and added a clause that required the business to pay his wife a large annual sum for as long as she lived. We didn't know how a failing business could stand up under the weight of all this. Our grown son came in to run it. He had a law degree and a business degree and after a few worrisome years he turned it around.

My father was failing. Although he had turned on me in fury, with mockery and insults, when I suggested that we buy out my brother, I still visited him and he still sat and held my hand and told me how sick my brother was. I don't know if he knew that my brother wasn't talking to me. I never told him. Ever since my mother's death, my father had changed, but a stranger wouldn't notice.

As to me and my brother - I felt that probably nothing but the terrible grief that we would share when my father died, would bring us together again. Only something as devastating as the loss of a parent would make him see how ridiculous it was for us to fight. What had we fought about? I didn't know, never having had words with him. He must have had a reason, real or perceived. And since the buy-out, he was living well and enjoying his life.

When my father's wife called to say that my father had suddenly fainted and slipped into a coma, my husband and I and our children flew to his bedside. It was evening when his wife met us at the hospital. I went alone to see him in the intensive care unit. He had tubes coming out of his body. He lay as though sleeping, breathing heavily. I sat beside him for a long time. I told him I had always loved him extravagantly. When I was a small child I thought he was a demi-God. He was brilliant, charismatic, kind, funny, handsome, loving, larger than life. Now he was an old man, my father. I don't know if he heard me. Tears were coursing down my cheeks as I emerged. I asked my father's wife if my brother and sister had seen him. They had come earlier, she said. They were staying with her, had departed the hospital before we arrived. *Tomorrow then*, I thought. *Tomorrow I will see them and we'll talk and grieve together, my brother, my sister and I and we will hug each other in our grief and perhaps become a family again.* The next morning I called my father's wife and told her we would meet her at the hospital.

"What time were you planning to be there?" she asked. I said I was not sure but soon.

"Why does it matter?" I asked.

"Because," she said, "your brother does not want to see you and asked me to find out when you were going."

So here it is ten years later. I never did reconcile with my brother. My sister and I remain close. She speaks to my brother and he to her. Our father died a day after our visit. My father's wife told me there would be no funeral. I began to organize a simple memorial service, but she called to say that I should cancel the arrangements, that my father would not have wanted one. Later I heard that she and my brother had held a memorial service to which I was not invited.

GOOD NEIGHBORS

Have you noticed all the excuses people have today? There was one kid I remember reading about, who killed one of his friends because the kid coveted his friend's sneakers. The kid's lawyer argued that the kid wasn't responsible. It was red dye number something or other, a food coloring, that made him do it. A man who killed his wife told the court between sobs that he adored his wife but he was sleepwalking at the time and therefore not responsible for cutting her throat. PMS has been used as an excuse for killing a rich husband. And one guy recently actually got off because he said he was drunk and didn't know what he was doing when he murdered someone.

I was different though. I didn't kill for greed - what do they say? - people kill for lucre, lust and something else, I forget what but it begins with an "L." I didn't kill for any of those things. I like to think I did it to make the world a better place. Whether or not that was my intention, I'm sure it is a better place with her gone. Maybe I did it to improve the garden. It certainly does look a lot better these days. The roses are the most beautiful red. Or maybe I was just exhausted.

In my case, like Lizzie Borden, I administered forty whacks - though not to my mother - and buried my neighbor in the garden. That was last November. It's now June and no one has missed her. No one has shown up at my door to ask questions and disturb the busy life of my family. My neighbor, you see, was running an illegal boarding house next door in an area zoned for single homes and when she didn't show up to collect the rent, her boarders surely noticed but they certainly never complained. She was so nasty I don't think there was anyone in the world who missed her. Even her creditors had given up on her, I imagine. And while I still don't have a green thumb, the roses are coming up beautifully in my garden for the first time. Morry is really surprised, but then he doesn't know about mulch - if that is the right name for it.

I'll tell you what happened.

I work in an office. It's a small business and I don't get paid much, but you could call me the Office Manager. I check the bills, enter them on the computer, write cheques, do the filing. Between my job and Morry's, we barely scrape by. We pay our bills like good citizens, but it's rough going. We dream of winning the lottery or something like that - I fill out every form promising me a fortune, even though I know they're all fake.

Here's an average day. Morry gets the kids up, lets Duma the dog out and then wakes me. Bleary-eyed I comb the knots out of Emma's hair while she screams. Then I try to get Maya to decide on an outfit for the day. Morry puts the kids' breakfast on the table while I shower and dress. I get downstairs just in time for him to kiss me good-bye and rush out the door. I let Duma in, grab a cup of coffee, stuff the kids into their snowsuits and drop them off at school before heading into the traffic for the long drive to the office. By the end of the day I'm usually so tired I can hardly hold my head up. In addition to non-stop work, I've already fielded at least three calls from the baby sitter calling to ask where to find a favorite toy or what to do about the cat that's gone missing.

I lock up the office at 5:30 and head home. The baby sitter takes off as though she were training for an Olympic class relay race. The kids are all hyped up, their toys strewn over the floor. The cat has reappeared and is throwing up on the kitchen floor and I have to start dinner.

Morry gets home at 6:30 looking like death warmed over. He is a contractor and has spent the better part of the day pleading with one of the trades to show up at the job. The rest of his time was spent supervising those that did show up and trying to collect from deadbeat clients. A lot of the time he's up there on the ladder doing some dangerous job himself because the carpenter hasn't shown up. If he doesn't get one area finished on time then the plumber or the carpet layer or the electrician can't begin. And if they can't begin on this house, they start on a new job and then, as Morry has explained to me many times, it's ball game over.

Anyway, Morry bathes the kids while I get dinner on the table. By the time the kids have had their last glass of water, have heard their last story and their favorite stuffed animal has been located behind the living room sofa or in the laundry basket, Mor and I are glassy eyed with fatigue. We shoo the cat off the bed before climbing wearily under the blankets. We read or watch TV until our eyelids can't stay apart and then the lights go out.

About 2 a.m. Em wanders into the room and climbs into bed. That lasts until one or the other of us can no longer stand being kicked repeatedly in the stomach. We end up dragging ourselves out of bed and carrying Em's inert form back into her own bed.

At 7:30 a.m. the whole thing starts again. On weekends things aren't much different except that the kids are now with us for the full twenty-four hours during which time we market, shop, walk the dog, take care of chores and repairs, go to the park, maybe even have someone else's kid over. It's exhausting even to talk about it. On Sunday mornings we take our kids to religious school so forget about sleeping in. As soon as we get back to the house it's time to pick them up again. Then we drive to my mother's house.

Does all this seem like an excuse for murder? You better believe it!

One day last winter the baby sitter called to say that the kids weren't feeling well and were crying, so I locked up the files, changed the message on the phone and rushed home early. There was a moving van taking up the entire space in the driveway we shared with our neighbor so I parked in the street and ran inside. A light snow was falling and the ground was slick. I slipped and fell heavily on a patch of ice by our front door. Limping inside, I tasted blood where I had bitten my tongue. The baby sitter took off to get to decathlon practice as usual, and I called the doctor and got her answering service. Morry was out of town on a construction job so I was on my own. I put the kids to bed and when they both fell right to sleep without asking for anything I got really worried. With motherhood you can't win.

It gets dark very early this time of year and the light was already fading. I peered out the window and saw that the moving truck was still blocking the driveway. I saw too that my car had been ticketed. I had agonized last weekend about replacing our crummy toaster - no pun intended. I needn't have bothered. That money would now go to the traffic bureau to pay for the police Christmas party. I felt anger and frustration but then I figured that the truck had to park somewhere and the new neighbor may not have known we shared the driveway. I went upstairs to check on the children. They were fast asleep. I felt their soft downy foreheads. They were both burning hot. I felt a stab of worry. The doctor had still not returned my call.

When the moving van finally left, I dashed outside without my coat, and drove back into the driveway. It was icy cold and my teeth were chattering. The snow made it difficult to maneuver. I saw my new neighbor came out of her house. I tried to smile as I prepared to welcome her to the neighborhood. We had always gotten on well with our former neighbor and having a shared driveway had never been a problem. There's plenty of room for two cars parked side by side and we had always cooperated with one another.

If there were guests we managed to squeeze them in. If one or the other of us found ourselves blocked, we had only to knock on the other's door and someone would come out to move the offending car. I had no reason to think that things would be different with this woman. I had no reason to think that our new neighbor would be different. But she was different. Was she ever! I rolled down my window to greet her but I didn't get very far. As the cold air streamed in and I shivered uncontrollably, she began to scream at me.

"Don't you know how to drive? Can't you see you're on my side of the driveway! If we're going to be neighbors, we'd better get some things straight right now." I didn't tell her about the ticket or the icy street, or the sick kids inside or the fact that I wasn't wearing a coat, I just backed up and drove in again, a few inches further to the left. The phone was ringing as I entered the house, my teeth chattering. Guess who? It was my charming new neighbor. This time she was outraged because she noticed that one of my kids had left a bicycle a few inches on her side of the driveway. I told her wearily that I would attend to it in the morning. That was not soon enough she told me.

"Look," I said, "I'm too tired to handle this nonsense. Your God damn moving truck filled the ENTIRE driveway all evening and I got a ticket. I'm holding you responsible for that!"

"In a pig's ear," said this neighbor from hell. "If you don't come right out and move that bike, I'm calling the police."

"Why don't you just do that?" I replied. "I'm sure they'll be delighted to take time off from catching rapists and drug dealers."

"Maybe I'll just drive over it," she said. By this time I was shaking with fury so when the doorbell rang, I was ready to kill her. We always keep Duma in the kitchen when there's someone at the door as she has a tendency to bark ferociously and tear out the front door terrifying anyone who doesn't know her. She's a fierce looking German Shepherd who wouldn't hurt a flea. But her bark is intimidating and she tends to jump on strangers in her eagerness to kiss their face. But this time when the doorbell rang I let her loose and then threw open the front door. She leapt on the figure that stood there in the waning light of a winter afternoon. The figure, a man, fell down heavily on the ice. Dimly I noticed the bunch of flowers that had flown out of the strangers' hand and were now strewn incongruously over the lightly powdered lawn. Dimly I noticed the initial smiles on the two accompanying figures turn to horror. One, a woman, was helping the fallen man to rise and the other, who was carrying a large movie camera began to film the scene.

Aghast, I sputtered, "I'm so sorry! I didn't realize...I thought it was ....." The three figures didn't stop for conversation. They practically ran back into the white van that had pulled into my neighbor's side of the driveway. As they drove away I noted the writing on the van. It said,"Publishers Clearing House."

That was when I decided to take matters into my own hands.

SWEET DREAMS

I'm tired. Just flat out tired. I'm still young - well, my kids think I'm old at forty-two. But there are dark territories under my eyes and grey streaks in what was once my pride and joy and is now a tangled mass of wiry cut ends. I run a bakery. I get up at 4 a.m. when the sky is still midnight black and the air bone-chilling cold, in order to get my ovens fired up for the day's bake. The shelves have to be filled with warm loaves of bread and the store smelling of freshly baked pastries when my customers start streaming - well, trickling - in for breakfast. Mid-morning I spend preparing sandwiches for the rush at lunchtime when the school kids come trooping in for a cheap meal.

Almost every day the bakery has a different variety of onanistic weirdo taking an opportunity to exhibit him or herself. Or perhaps some sad soul recently released from an institution to the tender mercies of the street, will start shouting that alien babies are being baked into our brownies. This causes the predictable mayhem and hysteria among customers and employees, until I come out of the kitchen to order him or her off the premises. I always feed a few of the panhandlers who come around though. I hate to see anyone going hungry.

The afternoon is spent cleaning up, entering data on the computer, calling in orders, soliciting catering jobs and sending off angry letters to our local MP about the municipal government's latest decision to select our busiest season in which to do road repairs in front of the store. I have to count and enter the days receipts and by 6 p.m., exhausted, I give final instructions to the night manager, drop the receipts off at the bank and head for the supermarket. From there I drag myself home to cook dinner for my husband and two teen-aged kids.

After dinner I work at my computer for a while, getting together new recipes, drawing up menus, figuring out the payroll for the following week.

The kids interrupt with such queries as, "Hey Mom, are you coming to the soccer game Thursday? I'm an alternate and might get to play this time!" or "Mr Baker is such a nerd. Will you see if I can drop History?"

I must admit that Howard is helpful with the dishes and puts things in the washing machine and other chores but I find it distinctly unhelpful when I am totally wiped out, to be told, "Honey, you look like a wet herring. I can't believe there is no one else in the store that can take the orders or scrub up!"

"Believe it, Howard. Just believe it," I say wearily.

Far from stopping him, he mutters, "Must be something wrong with the way you're doing things." Thanks Howard, thanks a lot.

Howard works hard too. He's in the same industry as me, only he's in admin and helps manage a chain of fast food outlets. That means he works all hours and often seven days just the way I do. He gets tired and discouraged too. I like to think that when he does, I try to boost him. But I'm probably too tired to notice.

After working at the computer I make a quick sweep of the house before falling into a hot tub. There's not much to do in the house. The kids are at school all day and their rooms are strictly off-limits to me. I never go near them. I am planning a visit after the kids have left for college a few years from now. In my imagination I see myself in Tilley pants and hat, presiding over what resembles an archeological dig - broken pottery shards, old implements, bits of food from years past hidden under mountains of detritus. I can even hear myself calling out, "Howard, come look. Eureka!" When Howard comes running I will triumphantly hold up the green Philips screwdriver lost so many years ago, and my plaid silk shirt which disappeared, oh, way back.

I often drift to sleep in the tub. Howard, thus far, has managed to waken me before, as he predicts, I slide under the waves. He is always warning me that one day he will arrive too late. Sometimes I think I won't care, I'm that tired. But I don't mean that of course. I have a wonderful family and an income we can scrape by on. That should constitute a good life, shouldn't it?

One day not too long ago, I took a few hours off and went shopping at the mall for clothes for the kids. I saw coming towards me an elderly woman. Her hair was greying and her face lined. She looked familiar but I couldn't quite recognize her until I got up close and realized I was looking into a mirror. That was a shocker.

Howard had been talking about going away for a few days, even threatening to go alone when I resisted, afraid of what would happen to the store without me. Suddenly I didn't care. I called him at his office.

"Honey, if you can get away, I'm ready to go."

"Are you serious? Cut the kidding."

"I mean it."

"Look, honey, I'd like to explore this sudden change in personality with you, but I'm about to go into a meeting with the TD people. Maybe we can talk about it tonight?" His voice was gentle and soothing, - altogether unlike him. I think he thought I was exhibiting signs of a nervous breakdown. But that evening I managed to convince him that I was as mentally alert as any person who has had less than six hours of sleep every night for the past year. We talked about where we should go. There were a multitude of possibilities. I was ready to go hiking on the Bruce Trail but Howard impatiently nixed that. He is not the outdoors type, and besides, as he explained, this was supposed to be a rest not a challenge.

"Y'know, I've been working pretty hard myself lately,"

I felt a stab of guilt as I noticed his tired eyes, the deepening lines etching a path from his thinning nose to the corners of his mouth, and saw, with a jolt of surprise that his hair seemed to be in retreat. Howard was no longer the young man I had married. He was middle-aged and worn down by trying to help his crazy wife make a decent living for their family, constantly anxious about the layoffs taking place all around him.

We settled for what promised to be a quiet sleep-filled weekend at a rustic country inn in the Rideau Valley. I made reservations at a place I'd heard about - Loon Lake Lodge. I wrote away for a brochure and received back colour photos of antique-filled rooms, large stone fireplaces, a small candle-lit dining room with flowers on each table. We would leave early on Friday. Maybe Howard and I could even - I mean if we're not still too tired by Saturday night, we might...you know.

The Lodge was about a four-hour drive. Howard took the wheel while I tried to stay awake, afraid that if I fell asleep he would too, and there would go our vacation. The ride seemed endless. I tried to make sprightly conversation, but Howard wasn't in the mood.

"Look at that cow. Doesn't he look picturesque standing there under that maple?"

"I don't find a cow pissing particularly picturesque."

"Who said he was pissing!"

"She was pissing."

"How do you know! You didn't even see her you were driving so fast."

"Not too fast to see that she was pissing." It was beneath my dignity to answer so I sunk back into a sulky silence. If this was the way our weekend was going to go....Why is it that when we go for a walk in the country, I see the cow and Howard sees the cow pie?

Finally we turned off the highway and after traveling a few miles on various side roads, found a quaint sign pointing to a pleasant driveway surrounded by large shade trees, their leaves in beautiful tones of yellow and russet. The lodge, set back from the road on a lovely lake, was charming. The weathered stone exterior covered by ivy, the low wood-beam entry with its plank floors, the paneled walls covered with old Confederation prints - everything was just what it should be, cozy and welcoming. It was an Eden that smelled of pine needles and tasted of maple syrup and blueberry pancakes. An Eden in which one heard the soughing of the wind and the call of the loon.

The owner, tall and skinny, was seated reading a magazine behind a tiny registration desk. He stood up, bending slightly so as not to hit his head, and stretched out a bony hand saying, "I give you welcome to the comforting splendors of Loon Lake Lodge."

Howard and I looked at one another, barely able to control our amusement. The adventure had begun!

We carried our luggage up a narrow stair to a door on which there was a brass plate reading"The King George Room" and entered.

We gazed at the mahogany canopied bed and hugged each other. A fire was blazing energetically in the old stone fireplace, despite the fact that it was October and the days were still warm. There were flowers and a few well worn books placed on the night table - Jeffrey Farnol and Willkie Collins. The room smelled of wood smoke. A distant loom called out to its mate. Howard and I stood there grinning foolishly at each other. Was this Heaven, or what?

I could have flopped down on the bed then and there and slept non-stop for forty-eight hours, but how much more wonderful it would be to look forward to that sleep after a long hot bath in the deep claw-foot tub, and a romantic dinner accompanied by several glasses of rich red wine in that candle-lit dining room with starched white table cloths and tiny vases of flowers. How much more wonderful it would be to rise from the table feeling an erotic lassitude creeping over my body, a heavy torpor overtaking my limbs, and make my way on Howard's arm back to the King George room, our King George room, and fall into our canopied bed, hearing the romantic call of a loon before falling into blissful sleep.

It was a little after ten when we climbed between those crisp white sheets and under the blankets. It felt doubly good as the room had taken on a bit of an autumnal chill, reminding us that winter was not far off. We tried to read for a while as is our custom, but our eyes kept closing. I switched off the bed lamp and turned to embrace Howard.

It was precisely at that moment that the nightmare began!

We both sat bolt upright in the dark. Rock music was literally pouring into our room - through the fireplace opening, the ventilator vents, through every knothole and pore of the old building, which seemed to be shuddering under the assault. The sound was blinding.

"What the hell is going on!"

I know myself. I must not get upset or my heart will start pounding and I will never get to sleep no matter how tired I may be. So I said, in what I hoped was a soothing voice, "Don't get upset. I'll call downstairs. Someone probably pressed the wrong button somewhere."

My call to the desk was answered by the owner who told me gravely that the music was no mistake, but rather a recently introduced and very successful marketing program called"Friday Night with the Inn Group," an effort to attract young people for drinking and dancing.

"What about us?" I demanded. "What about your hotel guests?"

"Do come join us," he intoned. "Let me offer you a glass of brandy in our disco." Disco!

"We are tired," I said. "We came here for a rest, not to dance. Can't you turn the volume down?"

"I'm sorry," he said haughtily. "I'm glad to offer you a brandy if you will join us in the disco, but I cannot lower the music."

"We came here for a rest, we are exhausted - we drove four hours!" My tone was a cross between a plea and an accusation. I heard myself becoming ever more shrill as, desperate with frustration, I cried, "We need sleep. Can't you at least give us a quiet room?" His reply was hardly helpful. He had given up on us and wanted to get back to his *Country Life* magazine.

"We have only eight rooms, and they are all occupied. In any case, none would be quieter."

"What about those comforting splendors, where the hell are they?" Howard had turned on the light and was pacing up and down with flames shooting from his eyes. At the top of his voice he shouted,"When is this God-damned music going to stop!" On the other end of the phone the Innkeeper heard the question and answered before I could repeat it.

"The disco closes at 2 a.m."

"You mean to tell me that this music is going to continue until two in the morning?" I shrieked. I think shriek is the proper description of my delivery of that question.

He simply repeated, "The disco, as I have said, closes at two," before I slammed down the phone.

Now my heart was beating furiously. I turned out the light again. We lay side by side, rigid with anger.

Speaking into the darkness, Howard said, "How the hell did you pick this place?"

I didn't want to believe he had said that. When blame was to attributed, who better than the person closest? I turned away, seething, trying to drown out the blare which even my own inner turmoil couldn't silence. Attempting to stop my ears to all unwelcome noise, I still couldn't help but overhear scraps of mutterings coming from the other side of the bed, mutterings such as, "...inconceivable that of all the places in the world we pick this crappy joint without making any inquiries," and "...how could anybody be so..." I missed the last word, but I could imagine several likely possibilities.

Unable to stand this double assault, I screamed at him above the din, "Oh great! Now on top of everything, blame has miraculously shifted, by some only too familiar but still mysterious mechanism, to me! It's my fault I suppose that acid rock is dripping into our ears." Tears were now running down my cheeks. "I have somehow engineered this dismal situation, either through sheer stupidity or is it simply my incredible ineptitude....or maybe you think I did it on purpose?" My voice was racked by sobs. "And what about you? Am I your God damned travel agent for God's sake? Why didn't you make inquiries? I suppose you know how to pick up the phone..."

Howard realized belatedly that he had gone too far, that I had reached my limit. He tried to take me in his arms, apologizing as he did so, but I was boiling beyond comfort. Now they were dancing downstairs, and in addition to the relentless beat of the music, there was a generalized thumping of feet which shook the entire building, something akin to the Calgary stampede. I don't know how long we lay on the bed in the darkness, stiff with fury. Even had we been able to blot out the music - and I must confess to having murderous visions of how that might be accomplished - we were now both so angry and upset there was no way we could sleep.

It must have been about 11 o'clock when Howard switched on the light, got out of bed and said, "I'm leaving." I wondered if he meant to drive off in the car abandoning me here, but not waiting to find out I jumped up. Throwing my night clothes in the duffel, I dressed in a flash. When we opened the door of our room, the sheer volume of what I can only derisively call music, practically drove us back inside.

The owner was still at the reception desk now talking with another guest. He looked up surprised to see us. "Ah, you have come to enjoy the mu ...." But when he saw our duffel he suddenly became galvanized. Emerging swiftly from behind the desk he ran after us calling out , "Just a minute.... your bill!" Howard made an inelegant reply having to do with the general location in which the owner might want to put - or more accurately - shove, the bill. The door slammed behind us.

As we walked to the parking lot, the night air was chill and suddenly quiet, eerily quiet, blissfully quiet. It took a few tries, but Howard got the car started up and soon we were back on the road headed for home. At first there was traffic, cars streaking by in the opposite direction leaving ribbons of light imprinted on our eyes. Then, as it got later, the roads became deserted. An early snow began to fall. It turned heavier, and as the flakes parted to let us through, I felt we were hurtling into nothingness. Dizzy with the need to sleep, I nonetheless was nursing my fury at Howard and at life and couldn't close my eyes. In any case, I dared not for fear that Howard too might fall asleep.

Now it was his turn to try to make conversation. "When d'you think we'll be home?"

"I have no idea."

"Do you want to try staying someplace else for the night?"

"Where did you have in mind?"

"I don't know. What do you think?"

"I've stopped thinking. Remember how bad I am at it!" I shouldn't have said that, but I couldn't resist. Howard gave up. We didn't speak further, driving in utter silence. My mind was lost in thought until those same thoughts led me circuitously to a new recipe I had left in my purse and my blood froze. My purse.

"Howard," I said in a very small voice. He didn't hear me, or if he did, he was not responding. "Howard," I said again, a bit louder.

"What?"

"We have to go back."

"We have to WHAT?"

"I forgot my purse in the room."

"You what?"

"I left my purse at the lodge."

Howard did not reply but drove straight on into the night for what seemed like forever, as if the enormity of what I had told him took time to be assimilated. Then, jamming on the brakes, he made a screeching U-turn on the now deserted road, throwing me wildly first one way and then the other. We headed back to the Loon Lake Lodge in what were the early hours of Saturday morning.

Neither of us said a word. I had nothing to say and was grateful that Howard said nothing. When we finally pulled into that familiar driveway, directed there by that same sign that had seemed so deliciously quaint on Friday evening a few miserable hours earlier, the lodge was shrouded in gloom. Snow was accumulating on the roof and window ledges. A dull light coming from somewhere in the interior served to heighten my feeling of dread. Howard drove up to the door, stopped the car and sat stolidly at the wheel, looking straight ahead into the night.

I didn't dare ask him to get my purse, though I did say meekly, "I guess you want me to go up?" There was no answer, so I climbed out of the car into the cold night. I was exhausted beyond comprehension. The freezing air revived me for a moment, but when I stepped into the now deserted reception area, the warmth of the building brought waves of fatigue crashing over me.

It was now well past 2 a.m. and the music had stopped, leaving no echo inside the ancient walls. All was silence except for the occasional creak and groan from the old building as it shifted its arthritic bones. I staggered up the stairs. The door to the King George Room was closed but unlocked. I entered stealthily feeling like a thief. Bed sheets and blankets were thrown about just as we had left them. Looking guiltily behind me, I shut the door. I didn't switch on the light but turned about looking for my purse in the soft glow left by the dying fire. After a moment of panic, I saw it lying where I had left it under the night table. I sat down on the bed and reached for it. The bed felt so good. I thought I would lie down for just a second...just a short second. My eyes closed and I fell into a delicious sleep. I sank deeper and deeper into heavenly unconsciousness.

In my dream I was throttling the tall skinny innkeeper. It was such a satisfying dream that I was affronted when interrupted in this important service. The lights suddenly blazed on and my shoulder was being shaken roughly. For a brief second before I recognized him through a haze of sleep, I thought Howard was a policeman come to take me off to wherever they take women stranglers. So it came as something of a relief to know that I wasn't about to be arrested. Howard's face looked worn and tired.

"Come on. Let's get out of here," was all he said.

I don't consider myself a violent person but I felt murderous. I do what I can to save the baby seals and whales and manatees and the dwindling numbers of rhino, but for a brief moment I felt driven beyond reason in my need to sleep again, to get back into that dream. Suddenly all the frustrations of my life welled up in me. The slovenly or dishonest employee. The unsatisfiable customer. The greedy landlord. The cheating supplier. The city fathers escalating their demands for tax revenues or establishing new building codes while tearing up the street in front of the bakery. Trying to be a good mother. Trying to be a good wife. Trying to pay the bills. The long days. The short nights.

For one brief but heavily freighted instant I felt myself capable of violence. But as I stared at Howard's worn and tired face, all the anger drained out of me. Howard was not to blame. Perhaps not even the innkeeper was to blame. Who then?

I stood up, took my purse and tip-toed down the stairs behind Howard, expecting at any moment to hear a shout of "Stop, thief!" But the lodge was quiet, the reception area deserted. Once outside, the night air felt cold but the car engine was running and it was warm in the car. Howard sat for a moment hunched over the wheel. He looked old and sad. I put my hand on his shoulder and said quietly, all the anger swept away, "Let's find a place to sleep."

We stopped on a dirt side road a few miles away, curled up in the car and slept like babies.

CALL FORWARD

I lived in a city apartment for a long time. It seemed the best and safest place for an unmarried working woman. It didn't look as though I was ever going to find the man of my dreams, so I had stopped dreaming. I had had flings in the past, but nothing worked out in the morning, so I had given up and was concentrating on my job. The city can be an exciting place for to live, and for an unmarried woman it offers more diversions than a small town. There are always concerts, plays or museum shows that one can go to with a girl friend.

My parents live in Phoenix, but they flew in for my big four-oh birthday. They stayed at a hotel, took me out to dinner and theatre and then flew back the next day. They didn't say a word about my still being unattached, but I could see it on their faces every time a young couple entered the restaurant. On my 41st, two gay guys from the office and an old school friend, Kay, took me out for a gala lunch. But other than that, life went on without too many milestones.

Then one day, all that changed. I had just gotten back to 527 Third, where I live, loaded with groceries, when Tim, the doorman, stopped me.

"Ms. Barry, can I ask you something?" he said awkwardly. From his embarrassed manner, I thought he was either going to ask me for a loan or if I knew that I had a stain on the back of my skirt.

"Of course, Tim," said I. He hesitated. He didn't seem to know how to begin so I added, "Just ask away."

"Well," he said, "I got a friend in the next building - you know, 529? He's the doorman over there and we got to talking and he told me - I don't know, maybe I'm stepping out of line here…"

"Tim, for Heavens sake, say what you have to say so I can get this food into the refrigerator." Luckily I didn't have ice cream but I did have some frozen foods - after all, what do singles eat? I couldn't see how a chat with the neighboring doorman could have anything to do with me unless they were planning an investment together that needed my active participation. Anyway, that got him talking and he told me that he had learned from his friend that this very nice single man in 529 walked his dog mornings and evenings and Tim's friend had said wouldn't it be nice if the man with the dog had someone who would walk with him. I frowned. Surely this wasn't what Tim had stopped me for?

Tim rattled on. He had told the other doorman that he knew just the person - an unattached, and, as he so tactfully put it, very attractive woman in his building, 527. So, between the two of them, they hatched up a plot to introduce me to Arthur Hamlin, a lawyer.

A lawyer? Was it desperation, amusement, curiosity or boredom that made me consent to this matchmaking? I don't know - maybe all of the above. In any case within the next few days I found myself looking at myself in the mirror as I arranged a colorful scarf around my neck and headed down to a liaison with a dog and his master.

Arthur Hamlin was standing in front of 529 talking to his doorman, but when I emerged he seemed to know whom I was. He and D.A. (I later learned that was for District Attorney, a nod to his profession) came to meet me. We introduced ourselves and it was love at first sight for D.A and me. He was a beautiful black lab, the really gentle kind with a soft head and soulful eyes. Arthur later told me that D.A.'s taste in women was infallible, and he had known immediately that his relationship with me was going t o thrive. And thrive it did. We walked in the park, talked about our jobs and found that we had a great deal in common, Arthur loved classical music and jazz, I love classical and folk - that was close enough. Neither of us had ever been married before, though Arthur had once been engaged, but his fiancée had died in a freak accident. That had been a long time ago, he said.

When we brought D.A. back to 529 that first evening, I waited downstairs while Arthur brought him upstairs. He reappeared shortly, after having hastily made a dinner reservation at a restaurant nearby. It all happened very quickly from there.

I don't have to describe my parents' jubilation when they heard I was getting married, and to a lawyer! Their happiness knew no bounds, but neither did mine. Arthur had a great capacity for love. He loved D.A. and he adored me. That was nice for me after so many years of living alone. He was a gentle man but he could be tough in the courtroom I was told. Still, he always tried to be fair. He didn't go for the jugular; he just wanted to get the bad guys off the streets and he managed that very well.

Both doormen, the matchmakers, Tim and Henley, came to our wedding, proud as punch, after which, Arthur and I settled into wedded bliss in 529. And it really was - wedded bliss, I mean. We were very happy together. We talked books and music; we went to concerts and ate in tacky little restaurants. On evenings when Arthur brought home files of work and took them into his study, I went to book club meetings or watched TV.

Of course we had our arguments. Some of the worst occurred when Arthur's first words on arriving home, were "What's for dinner?" as though he had married, not for life, but for dinner. I told him I didn't remember being elected cook, or was it my sex that automatically qualified me for the job? We got past that one, and now he helps, even with the marketing when he isn't too late getting home.

One of our worst arguments though happened like this. Arthur had a small sailboat that he liked to sail on a lake upstate during our summer holiday. When it was out of the water for the winter months, it sat in a sort of cradle. One spring morning, as the weather was beginning to become balmy with just a hint of chill left in the air, we drove upstate so that Arthur could get the boat ready to put in the water. As he climbed into the boat, still on the cradle, it tipped - Arthur fell out painfully and broke his leg.

With his leg in a cast, and on crutches, he was pretty helpless. He couldn't go to the office and I took leave from my office to take care of him. I waited on him hand and certainly foot. Because his crutches didn't allow him to carry anything in his hands, I had to be on call all the time. It seemed that every time I sat down, I would hear him calling, "Sandy, would you get me a glass of water?" or "Sandy, will you bring me my briefcase?" It went on like that all day long. I never said anything, but it would have been less than human not to feel some irritation, wouldn't it? In addition, I was doing all the marketing, the cooking, the cleaning, the dishes, the laundry, etc. while trying to keep up with my work on the computer. As time went on, his leg improved but it would still be a while in the cast, the doctor said.

One day when I got back from marketing, Arthur said proudly,"I did something for you today."

"Great!" I said merrily."What did you do?"

"I washed my underwear."

I thought that was funny, so I said,"You did something for me by washing your underwear? If you were going to do something for me, why didn't you wash my underwear?"

I was astonished by the passion of his fury. He had hobbled about to the hamper, managed to extricate his underwear (from mine) and put it in the washing machine. He had even managed to press the appropriate buttons on the washing machine so that it would start the wash cycle. How could I be such an ingrate? He was apoplectic with rage that I couldn't see the extent of the sacrifice he had made for me. I, in turn, was astonished by the reaction that my flippant comment had elicited. It took us a while to get past that incident. But we managed to, with our love for one another still intact.

Time flew by. We were all getting older, of course, but age hit D.A. the hardest. First his back gave out, and then his eyes. Finally, to the consternation of us both, he was diagnosed with cancer. On the weekends, we were constantly at the vet, consumed with worry. D.A. had been Arthur's companion for so many years, he couldn't conceive of living without him and I knew that, beyond feeling terrible for Arthur, I too would miss that big furry, lovable presence. But the day came when the vet said she could do no more for him, and that his pain was becoming unbearable. We had to put him down.

I was crying uncontrollably as I brought D.A. to the vet for the last time. I had taken a day off from work. Arthur couldn't bear to be there. The vet told me that the remains would be cremated - this was evidently done on a weekly basis - and that the ashes would be mailed to us in a padded mailer. We could if we wished, she said, come in later and select an urn. I had never been through the mechanics of losing a dog before, and it all seemed terribly macabre. I wept all the way home, and again as I told Arthur what the veterinarian had said.

Arthur is not a big man, but he is strong and compact. He has retained his hair and is still thin. But as I sadly told him about the imminent arrival of the padded envelope, which would contain D.A.'s ashes, his body sagged, his usually handsome face crumpled, and he looked ten years older. He was devastated and I could only hold him and try to comfort him. It is quite remarkable how bonded we can become to the quiet, gentle creatures who accompany us on our path through life, asking so little of us and giving us so much love in return.

Within a few days the padded envelope arrived. I set it gently on Arthur's desk next to a framed picture I had taken of him sleeping on the bed, with D.A. sprawled beside him with his chin on Arthur's head. There was another photo that had been taken when D.A. was just a young pup, frolicking with a Frisbee. I propped the envelope between the two photographs and that was where Arthur found it when he returned home late that evening after a particularly grueling day in the courtroom.

Arthur stayed in the study a long time and I left him alone there. When he emerged he had a strange look on his face.

"What is it?" I asked.

"You'll think I'm crazy."

"No I won't. Why should I think you're crazy? Nothing could make me think that!" When he remained quiet, I said again, "Tell me what's bothering you. I won't think you're crazy, I promise."

He began very hesitantly. "I was looking at those pictures of D.A. and remembering all the endearing things about him - how he would lick my face in the morning to get me to take him out, how hysterical with joy he would be when I came home as if he thought he would never see me again - even if I was gone for only five minutes."

"Yeeeeees…" I said, trying to encourage him to continue.

"You won't think I'm crazy?"

"No! I told you I wouldn't!"

"Okay then, here goes. ….D.A. called me."

"Called you," I repeated. "Called you. You mean like, 'Yoo-hoo,

Arthur?'"

This man is crazy, I thought. *He's flipped his lid; He's gone buggy. He's off the trolley tracks. Missing some buttons. His porch light has gone out. His grief has stopped the elevator from reaching the top floor.*

"Don't make fun of me," Arthur said. "I know dogs don't talk. You promised not to think I'm crazy but I can see…"

"No, no." I said, "I just don't understand. How was he calling, barking?"

"No, calling."

"You mean like, um, on the telephone?"

"Like on a cell phone, yes. Don't look at me like that, I know it's crazy and it couldn't have happened, but it did."

"Him. You mean the ashes, they were calling you."

"Ummm…"

"Did you answer? What were they, or he, saying?" My grammar was getting confused, but then, so was I. "Did he say where he was calling from? Doggie Heaven?"

This got Arthur angry. I had gone too far. He turned on his heel and went into the bedroom and shut the door. He had never done that before. Things were very quiet the rest of the evening although I tried to apologize. I knew he was under tremendous stress and I shouldn't have made light of his - his, what? Visitation? But it really worried me.

And when I get really worried, my only reaction is a sort of hysterical laughter.

The next morning, Arthur apologized. "I must have been crazy last night," he said. "Everything just got to me."

"Forget it," I said. "You loved D.A. so much, I can understand how…how you wanted to hear him again, see him again. Why don't we go out to dinner tonight, and, I don't know, just have a romantic evening, if we can"

He nodded, and so it was that evening that we found ourselves in an expensive little restaurant around the corner from our apartment. Arthur was still very low, and I was having trouble cheering him up.

I kept thinking of D.A. punching the numbers in his cell phone from Doggie Heaven somewhere, and I would feel a bit of hysteria rising in my throat, which I could only douse by looking extra mournful. I loved D.A. too but the idea that he was trying to contact us on his Nokia was a bit much.

Dinner was not a great success. The next morning we both left for work together. I got home before Arthur, as I usually did, and was preparing dinner when the phone rang. It was the vet. She sounded breathless.

"There's been a terrible mistake," she said. My mind began racing as minds do when someone says something alarming like that. But what kind of terrible mistake could come from the vet? I said the only thing that came into my head.

"D.A. is still alive?" I ventured tentatively.

"No, no. D.A. died very peacefully."

"Thank goodness for that. Then what?"

"His ashes." Uh oh.

"Did you send us the wrong ashes?" I asked in some relief. After all, if we had the wrong ashes, then it was some other dog communicating with Arthur from Doggie Heaven, perhaps just trying to tell him that they got their ashes crossed.

"No, you see it was the cell phone."

"What about the cell phone?" Now it was I who was going crazy. Was she going to tell me that the ashes had called her too from a cell phone? I heard her voice through a fog as she continued.

"My phone wasn't working right. I decided to return it in a padded envelope. My secretary got the addresses confused so your padded envelope has…"

"No ashes. A cell phone," I finished for her.

D.A.'s ashes had been sent off for repair. I tried to imagine the reaction of the person who opened the envelope in the repair department of the company. And once again, I felt hysteria rising. But I managed to comfort the vet and hang up as quickly as I could, thanking her for her call.

What was I going to say to Arthur? He hadn't been crazy after all. His porch light was still on. His trolley was firmly on the tracks. His elevator was reaching the top floor.

But if I told him the truth, he might have decided that he was crazy to have thought it was D.A. calling.

When he came home that evening, I didn't mention D.A. But after dinner, Arthur said he'd been thinking about it, and he thought we should select an urn. Maybe he hoped that would stop the incoming calls. Thinking quickly, I said the first thing that popped into my mind - that D.A. was such a big dog, he might feel confined in a tiny urn. Arthur looked at me strangely as if he thought I was making fun of him, but then seeing I was serious, he said, "Okay, we'll leave things as they are."

And that is why, a cell phone, with its battery now mercifully dead, sits in a padded envelope on Arthur's desk to this day, between the two photographs of D.A. in happier days.

THE ALIBI

I'm a guy who hates to make mistakes, y'know what I mean? Sure, everyone makes mistakes sometimes, but I try real hard not to and I usually don't. Now marrying Mary Lou was one helluva big mistake, though at the time I had it all planned out. Who would have guessed that her millionaire old man would write her out of his will when she married me? What kinda unnatural father is that, I ask you? I coulda done a lot for the old man if he'd taken me into his business like I planned, but he got mad and sold the whole damn thing and left the money to some religious charity. They sure took him for a sucker! I coulda told him something about those religious types.

Okay, so I made a mistake with Mary Lou, the old cow. But this time I knew I had it all planned out right. It happened by accident, see. I went skiing last winter. Mary Lou didn't go of course. She can hardly pull herself out of bed. There on the slopes I see this vision of beauty and what a skier! The guys can't take their eyes off her, and then she falls down right in front of me! I pick her up, dust her off and invite her for a drink. She accepts and that's how I met Vikki! She's got this big rock on her finger and anyway from the way she's dressed I can tell that she's loaded. She tells me her old man sells guns and tanks and things all over the world, and they're descendants of some royal house or other in Europe. I'm impressed I can tell you. I don't want to tell her I'm just a sales rep for HiRi Industries so I make like I'm some big executive. We hit it off, know what I mean? We spend a lot of time together and not just on the slopes.

It certainly didn't hurt that Vikki had it all - the cheek bones of some high fashion model along with the wealth of the landed European aristocracy. Her great grandfather had even had pretensions to the crown of Montenegro, but with the good sense to keep his assets in Switzerland. The family had long since moved -first to Germany and then after the great war, to the United States.

Since restoration of the monarchy in Montenegro seemed like a losing proposition, the family entered into the highly lucrative legitimate, if slightly shady field of international armament sales. They knew everyone of importance and influence - a big boost to my business schemes.

So it's clear. The first thing I gotta do is get rid of the old cow. A plan incorporating murder and promotion -and no mistakes- is boiling in my head, and when I set myself to do something, I do it for real.

I'm seein' Vikki on the side and there's no harm in usin' her name to get me the position I oughta have. So I tell my boss - his name is Molnar, George Molnar - that I got this friend and her old man is into munitions and very rich and influential and maybe could help out with some of the big time financing he's trying to drum up. And maybe with his connections, her old man could even get the crazy environmentalists off Molnar's back. Molnar's really got a thing about those weirdos who are always throwing a monkey wrench into his development plans.

Well, Molnar really lights up. I can tell it hurts him to say it, but he tells met I'd be in line for a promotion and maybe a raise if the loan came through because of me etc. and like that. So I arrange a "business dinner" at some fancy restaurant, and I bring Molnar to meet Vikki and her father. The meeting is a great success. The first order of business is accomplished!

I know I don't have to tell you what the next order of business was. I hadda get rid of Mary Lou. There was no way she woulda divorced me even if she caught me in flagrante delicious or whatever. I coulda sued to divorce her, I suppose, but I had a better idea. I knew she had a life insurance policy - we both did, and I could use the money. So I decided to dispose of Mary Lou in a way that no one would ever suspect me. I cooked up a great idea.

I began to let people know with tragic looks and dark hints that they couldn't miss that Mary Lou had a lover. Who would want that bag? In any case, I couldn't've cared less. But I played the part of the tragic Romeo to the hilt, with just the right blend of guilt-ridden soul-searching and stricken bitterness.

Molnar really looked surprised when I told him.

"Ah," he said, "how sharper than a viper's tooth is a woman's betrayal." I don't know what the hell he was talking about, but I knew he would remember what I'd told him.

To Fern Birchwood, my secretary, I muttered, as she began turning off lights and locking files for the evening, "What's the point of going home when no one cares?" She shot me all kinds of sympathetic looks.

Next I announced that I was going off into the woods, deer hunting, to take my mind off my troubles by communing with nature. Hah! I even asked everyone's advice on what type of gun I should buy. I joined a rifle club and I was really good at shooting! I got these great reflexes and an "unerring eye" the instructor tells me.

I'm building my alibi, see, block by block. How could anyone seriously accuse me, Millard Baxendale of premeditated murder when I'm so open about what's goin' on, so real proud about my gun? If I was a man with murder on his mind I'd have to be crazy to tell everyone I knew about my wife's goings-on, wouldn't I? An' I told everyone about the gun that I kept in the garage, so it would be easy to claim that an intruder discovered it and killed her when she found him.

I imagined myself a policeman and then a psychiatrist. Naturally the first person they would suspect would be the husband. But I intended to have an iron-clad alibi - Vikki would say I was with her - but beyond that it would be so clear to anyone who gave it thought, that if Millard Baxendale had planned to kill his wife in cold blood, it would not be with his own rifle. That was too laughable. He couldn't be that stupid. Right? And if he was going to kill her in a moment of passion, it was ridiculous to think that this would happen in the garage. I had it all figured out. The police would expect a crime of passion to take place with any instrument that came to hand and inside the house.

It was nearing double "M" day. "M" for murder and "M" for Mary Lou. By this time, there was so much gossip going around concerning the Baxendales, gossip that I had started, that it didn't come as too much of a shock to everyone when Mary Lou was found dead, brutally murdered. It was a shock, of course, to Mary Lou. But you gotta believe me - and here's the weird part - the biggest shock was to me! That's because Mary Lou wasn't murdered on "M" day but on "M" day minus one. Moreover, she'd been bludgeoned with an andiron in the bedroom and it was me who found her for God's sake. In one way I was glad, but a part of me was miffed that I'd never had a chance to work out my scheme.

I'd spent the evening at Vikki's place, careful as always, making sure that no one had ever seen me and Vikki together. When I got home I poured himself a drink in the living room, glanced through the evening paper and then went upstairs to where I imagined I'd find the cow asleep. Instead I discovered the body sprawled across the bed covered in blood. I gotta admit I completely lost my normal cool. I felt shocked and betrayed. Wasn't this just like the old cow to go and get herself killed like this just when I...

I dialed 911. The police arrived. Where had I been all evening? I had to confess about Vikki - after all she was the only one to have seen me that evening. This time the alibi was for real. We had been together all evening, drinking martinis while someone was clubbing Mary Lou to death. Naturally they checked with Vikki. That was when things started to go wrong. The police told me about their interview with Vikki. She had a memory lapse. Yeah, she said, she remembered she'd met someone called Millard Baxendale on the ski slopes. She said she remembered that he made an awful nuisance of himself after that. He was a married man she said and not only that, a salesman! He wanted to go on seeing her, she said, but she'd turned him away. "Why were they interested in all this past history?" she wanted to know. "What happened?"

At my trial, the judge asked me if I had anything to say so I gave an impassioned speech, explaining to the stupid jerks in the jury that if I wanted to get rid of my wife I would do it in the garage with my rifle like it was supposed to be, not in the bedroom with a blunt instrument. The jury listened but I couldn't tell nothin' from their faces. They found me guilty by reason of insanity and I was sentenced to be committed to a high security mental institution. By that time I was mad all right, but not so mad that I couldn't read the papers. George Molnar married Vikki and whadd'ya know the next thing I read is that HiRi gets a big loan from somewhere and Vikki's father gets to be Chairman of the Board.

FACING THE FACELESS

BUREAUCRACY

I shouldn't have made the illegal left turn, but my daughter, Emma, had an abscessed tooth and I had to get her to a dentist as quickly as possible. The policeman materialized out of nowhere. He sympathized as he went on writing out the ticket.

The following day I went to traffic court to plead "Guilty with an Explanation." I try to schedule my days so that I can get my work done but even in the best of times, this is difficult and stressful. It involves a long day at the office going over countless accounts, making phone calls, picking up fifty 'important' email messages, rushing out to get the kids when my wife can't, and sharing the household chores. My days really don't allow for trips to traffic court, so I took a dim view of the long, slow-moving line on which I would be obliged to stand in order to make my explanation. I suppose they do this so you will get tired of standing and just decide to pay the fine. But I was determined to try to make my case. It had been an emergency with a weeping child in great pain.

It took an endless forty-five minutes to reach the front of the line when I found myself standing finally before the only window open for business. I presented my ticket, which was duly stamped by a bored looking clerk with an ordinary date stamp and handed back to me.

"You will be receiving a letter marked 'Important Message,' ignore it," I was told. "Some time later you'll receive the date of your court hearing."

"I had to wait forty-five minues to be told that?" I asked irritably. "Couldn't there be a posted notice or something?" The woman just stared at me and said, "Next!"

I rushed back to my office to catch up on missed work.

In due time I received the letter marked "Important Message." It stated that if my fine was not paid within ten days a warrant for my arrest would be issued. Putting my admittedly shaky faith in the word of the clerk, I ignored this "important" and intimidating message and awaited the arrival of the letter which would inform me of the date of my court hearing. This came on April 1. My court date was set for the evening of April 2. I was stunned. Important personal considerations made that time impossible. I examined the envelope. I couldn't fault the post office - the notice had been mailed only on March 29th.

Once more I rushed to the traffic court. Once more there was only one window open for business and about thirty people waiting on line. A quick computation told me if each person took only three minutes to finish his or her business, I would still be waiting over an hour and a half. I looked about me frantically. Over there, with a shade pulled down, was a window marked "Inquiry." I could hear voices coming from behind the window, so I knocked on the glass. No response. I knocked louder. A disembodied voice said, with irrefutable logic, "There's no one here."

"I just have one simple question."

"There's no one here," the reply came back. "Go around to the window on the left." Relieved that there was an alternative to the long and slow-moving line, I headed left. There was no open window to be seen. Back I went to the shaded Inquiries window and once again banged on the glass. A clearly irritated voice said from behind the shade, "What is it?"

"There is no window to my left."

"I didn't mean to your left," the voice replied. "To my left."

To her left? There was only the long line snaking forward at a snail's pace. I was defeated by the quite literally faceless bureaucracy and took my place meekly at the end of the line. Fifty-five minutes later there was one man ahead of me who had come for his court hearing only to find his name not on the docket.

I noticed that although she had a computer, the clerk never consulted it. Behind her, file drawers stood open in obvious disarray.

Piles of tickets were held together with rubber bands. The clerk now disappeared for fully five minutes. I don't suppose there is anyone who doesn't recognize the scene - having been standing for what seems hours, just as you get to the head of the line, something happens - the computer crashes, the adding machine is out of tape, it's time for the salesperson or teller or postie to take his or her lunch break. I have toyed with the idea of writing a book about all the things that can happen as you approach the front of a line.

At long last it was my turn. I told the woman my problem.

"You can't change a date," was the curt reply.

"What do you mean I can't?"

"You can't change the date of a court hearing," was the implacable response.

"But this is completely unreasonable! I received this notice today and it calls for a hearing tomorrow night."

"I am sorry, but..." she started once again.

I interrupted, "It is unreasonable in the extreme to mail a notice on Friday for a court hearing for four days later! Look when it was mailed!" I waved the letter in front of her. I got her attention. She disappeared and returned with a supervisor who doubtless had been hidden behind that closed shade. "It's unreasonable..." I was saying again in something between a plea and a shout, when, peering at the letter she announced triumphantly, "You have been given ample notice, Sir. If you will take the trouble to look at the date carefully, you will see that your court date has been scheduled for April 2, one year from tomorrow!" I was stopped in my tracks!

"You mean to tell me that my court date has been scheduled for one year from now?" I asked in disbelief, not knowing whether to laugh or to cry.

"That's right," she said," all court dates are being scheduled a year from now." She turned back to her important work of turning people away from behind the closed shade. I slumped out of the building completely demoralized.

The following day my wife, went to the Small Claims Court offices in the same building to find out how to file a claim. After having heard my story and witnessed my frustration, she was relieved to see no line at all. In this room there was only a single clerk sitting at a desk. The clerk didn't look up or make eye contact. Her single concession to having noticed the presence of my wife was to lower her voice as she continued to speak - now in a whisper - into the phone.

My wife stood there...and stood there....and stood there. Finally, the clerk hung up, immediately turned her back, and reaching into her purse extracted a bottle of orange juice, which she proceeded to pour it into a cup on her desk.

"Excuse me," my wife said. "I am waiting."

The woman didn't turn around but yelled out into the void, "Someone's waiting."

After a few minutes a young woman emerged from the dim recesses of the back office. Perfectly pleasant, polite and helpful, she told my wife that if she wished to file a claim she must first obtain and read the government booklet on how to file a small claim. In response to my wife's request for the aforementioned booklet , this woman explained that none were available anywhere as they were out of print.

Franz Kafka would feel perfectly at home in the modern world.

THE GENDER GAP

On Sunday evening, Harold and I drove directly to the airport to pick up Noah. It had been our habit, on driving down from the country, to visit Harold's mother, now elderly and alone, and then go straight home. This change from our usual routine made Harold testy and irritable. Harold does not take kindly to breaks in our pattern.

After thirty years of marriage, Harold and I have come to share some remarkably similar attitudes, but our temperament, our way of handling problems, remains remarkably dissimilar. For instance, Harold would be delighted to learn that, due to some miracle, all the peoples of the earth were suitably fed, housed and clothed, and living under various benign forms of government. Moreover, he would be willing, if correctly approached, to make a substantial contribution toward that end. When he learns, however, and not to his surprise, that the world is not so ordered, he does not feel an overwhelming obligation to change things.

I, on the other hand, feel a sense of responsibility and obligation toward everything, often to a foolish and illogical degree. The expressions, "There but for the grace of God....." or "Cast thy bread upon the waters..." are not mere abstractions to me. Moreover, it is not simply my duty to help. I want to help. The way others might covet a diamond ring or a new car, I covet an opportunity to be of service, to help.

It was overcast as we approached the airport, and the first drops of rain, large and lazy, splattered against the windshield as we drove into the immense covered parking lot. Construction on the highway had caused traffic to back up, and we had not a moment to spare as we hurried down the ramp from the garage to the terminal building.

Harold's back was bothering him again, so I ran ahead, my overstuffed purse swinging wildly at my side. Large ceiling-hung television monitors announced arrivals and departures. I fumbled through a mass of detritus in my purse, trying to locate my glasses. What was Noah's flight number? I could not remember. He was coming a long distance - from Indonesia - and was booked on Air France. But now I realized in confusion, that I did not know where the last leg of his journey had originated. How were we to find the right gate?

The average big city terminal building is not designed to make life easy for the uninitiated. There was no Information Center anywhere, no signs directing the bewildered, nor were there any clearly identifiable personnel to whom one might address a question. All about us were hordes of people, puzzled, bored, hostile or eager. But we saw no one who could answer our queries.

There were several Air France flights scheduled to land at about the same time, so we darted from gate to gate, searching the weary faces of incoming passengers. In such a situation, I am apt to become so unstrung that I doubt my ability to recognize even a close friend. Could that be he? I started to call out and then stepped back in embarrassment as the man in question turned to stare at me.

The terminal was cavernous, and on Sunday evenings during the summer, it is usually filled with perspiring humanity from all over the globe. Passengers from incoming flights were succeeding one another with bewildering rapidity. It was very easy to miss someone there even when standing at the correct gate. Not knowing the exact flight number, Harold and I stood alternately at different gates, sometimes together, sometimes apart, scanning each face.

Another fundamental difference in our temperaments would now have been immediately obvious to anyone interested. I take the buffeting of fate and the stupidity of mankind as natural forces, similar to earthquake or flood, catastrophes against which it is useless to rail. Harold, however, fights back with all the weapons at his command. These include an arsenal of curses, imprecations, rhetorical questions, and a general undifferentiated irritability directed at anyone unfortunate enough to be near. Due to the nature of our relationship, this unfortunate individual is likely to be I.

And so when Noah did not appear at any gate, when waiting

families had eagerly greeted friends and relatives as they emerged from under the pewter gaze of the Customs official, and hurried off into the night, Harold and I found ourselves suddenly deserted in that vast reception area. Harold's mood swung the gamut from irritable to irascible. I found myself bombarded with rhetorical questions which, in my view, did nothing to shed light on the situation.

"Why the hell couldn't he just have taken a cab in the first place? Whose brilliant flash of inspiration brought us out here?" I preferred not to answer, nor was I impressed by the literary allusion contained in the next question.

"Jesus Christ! Jason never would have made it to the golden fleece if he'd had to go through this maze."

A mutual silence descended upon us, along with the certainty that Noah must have gotten past us somehow, and gone to town on his own. In fact, he might now be comfortably settled in our apartment, while we waited here in the muggy, moist night.

The rain had softened to a fine mist as we crossed the roadway leading back to the parking garage. A steel buggy, of the type found at supermarkets and used at the airport to transport luggage, stood deserted at the ramp. A lone, slightly sodden case sat in the basket. I stopped walking. Harold continued on.

Standing my ground, I said, "Someone has left luggage here." Harold did not even turn around. "Harold! It will be stolen."

Harold turned slowly and stood looking at me, warily.

"We have to find the owner!"

The exasperation in Harold's tired voice was measured, sarcastic and familiar. "How do you propose to do that?"

I paused but for a second before answering,"We have to take it to the Lost and Found."

The triumph in my voice made Harold realize, too late, that he had made a tactical error in assuming that this problem was too much for me. He tried to recover lost ground.

"Has it occurred to you that someone may have deliberately left it here, planning to come back for it later?"

"Ridiculous," I said. "Why would someone do that? It will be stolen if we just leave it here."

"Can't you let anyone take care of their own life? Must you always feel that you have been placed on this earth to save people from their own mistakes?" Harold stormed. But I had already grabbed the case and was hauling it out of the buggy with a determination reserved only for such occasions. Harold glared at me. He turned to walk off alone to the parking garage. I stood staring at his back, feeling damp and unsure. Surely he would not leave me here alone?

After four or five steps, Harold stopped and slowly faced me. He had been walking a bit unnaturally. His back was evidently bothering him again, filling me with guilt as he said with a kind of world-weary and infinite patience, as though talking to a small child - or an idiot, "Are you really planning to take that bag?"

My courage returned by this show of interest, I boldly replied with an assurance that I did not feel, "I must take it to the Lost and Found." Then shifting to the first person plural, and with a pleading note clearly detectable in my tone, "We have to. We can't just let it be stolen. After all, if it were ours and we had inadvertently left it..."

Harold know this train of thought from past experience. He interrupted with "Christ!" and then, "All right, Let's get this thing over with."

Harold's bark is always worse than his bite and I have come to rely on his essential generosity of spirit.

We walked back into the terminal building. The Arrivals area stretched for miles. We asked a lonely porter for directions. He scratched his head and leaned upon his baggage carrier as he suggested that we try upstairs in the Departures Area. He pointed vaguely into the distance and we walked on, threading our way through scattered knots of people, noticing no one.

The case was not heavy. It seemed to be a cosmetics bag or jewelry case. Still, it was awkward to carry. As we finally neared the escalator at the far end of the building, I stumbled over the strap, spilling the contents of my purse onto the glassy floor. Round the feet of passersby skittered pencils, pens, pins, tape measure, lipstick, coins, papers, notebook, credit cards, photos, tampons...

Under Harold's furious gaze I scrambled about, collecting my things. I dimly heard his imprecations, his calls to an omnipotent presence to wreak havoc on this scene; his rhetorical questions addressed to an unseen onlooker, demanding an explanation of why he had allowed himself to be dragged into this ridiculous misadventure; his ominous predictions of permanent back injury leading to his total incapacitation. His choice of vocabulary was direct, explicit, and to me, unseemly. But I did not dare to expostulate.

The escalator was broken so we were forced to mount its stubbornly high and rigidly unrelenting steps. Panting we reached the top and looked about us for a sign leading the weary traveler to the Lost and Found, or for some uniformed or simply informed person to whom a desperate question might be addressed. None of these seemed to exist.

By now I could see by the warning look in his eyes, that I had tried Harold's patience to its uttermost limits. I stopped at the ticket counter of a small feeder airline, described our predicament to the pretty, young ticket seller, and when she too was unable to tell us where to find the Lost and Found, I threw myself upon her mercy, begging her to take the bag into her care.

"See," I told her, "it has a label on it. Mrs. Mary Chernowski, 478 Mercer Street in Hamilton ... Won't you please be good enough to see that ...My husband has a bad back..."

She furrowed her brow as she tried to remember where the Lost and Found might be, and then, failing, agreed to take the bag into her care. I was filled with an overwhelming love for that young woman.

The long walk back to the parking garage was a silent one. I knew enough not to disturb Harold's moody introspection. I held my purse tightly, lest it betray me again. Harold was walking with a pronounced limp by the time we reached the formerly deserted Arrivals area again. Now it was crowded with people once more. They were, the monitor told us, meeting an Alitalia flight from Milan. Expectant voices speaking in a lyrical tongue that I did not understand, made me feel suddenly terribly alone.

Noah was still nowhere to be seen. Surely he had taken matters into his own hands long since. He would be home, no doubt, wondering what had become of us.

We walked outside again. It had gotten quite dark and the arc lights were on. As we approached the ramp, we could see lights reflected in the pool of water in which the single luggage cart still stood. Around it, a small elderly woman was circling and recircling. Her head was uncovered and tiny droplets of rain caught in her spidery hair net. She was clutching and unclutching her hands. As we approached, she said quite clearly, "Oh what could have happened to it? I only left it for a few minutes..."

SIGHT UNSEEN

The sign read, "All Are Welcome Here Regardless of Age, Sex, Creed or Colour," but he didn't even look at it. He stumbled slightly as he crossed the threshold into the big noisy hall filled with chattering voices and loud music.

A woman's voice made itself heard over the din, "Have I seen you here before? No? Well you are welcome any Saturday night. You can check your things right here. The refreshment bar is in the back and over to your left. I'm so glad you came. If you'd like to dance, you'll find many attractive ladies who will be delighted I'm sure. Would you like me to introduce you to..."

"No," he said gruffly. "I want a drink first."

"That's fine," she said, swishing off, "just walk straight back for refreshments."

He headed for the bar through crowds of people. He hated crowds. He was sorry he had come. What could he find here to ease his fierce anger, approaching despair? At the bar he growled, "Gimme a beer."

"Sorry, Sir, we have only soft drinks."

"Then give me a goddam Coke!"

A woman standing at the bar turned to face him, asking in a soft voice, "Do you need a beer all that bad?"

He turned around, liking the sound of her voice. "I don't like Coke," he said, his voice softening somewhat, but still impatient.

"Then why not have a lemonade? They make them here and they're really good."

"You must come here a lot."

She laughed. "This is my second time. A cousin of mine dragged me here the first time. By the way, I'm Edna Bates. How do you do?" They shook hands.

"Would you like to dance, Edna Bates?" he asked.

"Sure would," she said taking his hand. As they walked onto the dance floor, he called over his shoulder to the bar tender, "No sale this time, Mac."

"They don't make money on the drinks anyway so he doesn't care." Her laugh was lovely. He put his cheek against hers as they began to dance. Her skin was soft.

"You know all about this place, don't you?"

"No."

They danced silently for a while and then he said, "You from around here?"

"I live in Toronto now but I wasn't born here. I was born in Arkansas."

"Really?" His voice became animated for the first time. "I'm from Louisiana. Christ, I miss the smell of the sea."

"Why don't you go back?"

"Why don't you?"

"I didn't say I missed it."

"Don't you?" The music had stopped for a few minutes and they stood there in the middle of the dance floor holding hands. He asked the question as though in the answer lay a clue to his own desperation.

"Sometimes I do I guess. I miss our small town where we kids used to run around barefoot in summer. I loved the feeling of the dust between my toes. I loved the feeling of knowing everyone as though they was all my kin. I felt free there as a kid. But when I grew up, I didn't feel free anymore. I felt stifled. After my mother died I came here. How about you?"

His voice was charged with bitterness as he replied, "I was serving in the armed forces and I had an accident. Just a goddam accident! They shipped me to a hospital and I stayed in there for almost two years. When I got out, I couldn't go home again. There was nothing left there for me. I've been batting around ever since."

"I'm sorry."

There was a long silence between them. The music started again. She waited expectantly until he broke the silence.

"You want to dance some more?"

"Sure, if you do. I love to dance."

"You're good at it too. C'mon."

As they glided across the floor she asked, "You have a job?"

"Yeah. I work in a furniture factory. Before I joined the Service I wanted to be an engineer."

"Did you go to college?"

"No."

"Why? Couldn't you afford to?"

"Oh I could afford to all right. My folks would've been glad to send me. But I enlisted right from high school and after I got out of the hospital there was no more school for old Buddy Boy here."

"Why?"

"What the hell do you keep asking me 'Why' for?"

"Sorry."

"How could I go back to school? It was too hard. I couldn't concentrate anymore. And what was the point in just learning things. It was too late to be an engineer."

"I wish I could have gone to school and learned something. Anything at all. But we couldn't afford that. I started working when I was still a kid."

"Where do you work now?"

"I'm in telephone sales."

"Let's go back for that drink."

"Okay. Try the lemonade this time." They laughed and he held her hand.

"I never came to this place before."

"I know."

"Yeah, well I never even been to a dance hall before."

"This isn't exactly a dance hall," she said with laughter in her voice, "It's sort of a club."

"Some club!"

"It is! They're really nice people who run it. They're trying to help us...the lonely people...to find friends."

"You lonely?"

"Sometimes. Most of the time."

"How about your cousin?"

"Oh Ruby - she just came up from Arkansas for a few days. She's married to a guy from there. She found out about this place and dragged me here. She's going back tomorrow."

"My parents died while I was in the hospital and I lost track of all my old friends. What would they want with me now anyway?"

"You do yourself an injustice. Why wouldn't they want to see you again?"

"It's too late."

"Too late for what?"

"I'm not the same person I once was. I wish I just had one more crack at the can - you know what I mean? One more chance to do things right."

"You can make that chance. Why not?"

He thought, *Maybe you're that chance*, but aloud he said, "How about us going somewhere for a beer?"

"Thanks, but I can't. Ruby'll be here soon to pick me up."

"Why? Can't you go home alone?"

"I'm afraid to. That's one thing I miss about home. I wasn't afraid to go anywhere alone. It's funny. There are good things and bad things about a big city."

"I don't know the good things, but I sure know the bad."

"Are you very lonely?"

"I don't know..."

"I know you are...just being with you and listening to you talk! You sound as if you're as unhappy as it's possible to be."

"What's that to you?"

"Nothing. Only I've been through it too."

"Are you doing anything tomorrow night?"

"No."

"Would you like me to pick you up at your place and maybe we could go somewhere together? I'll bring you home."

"Are you sure you want to?"

"What the hell!" he exploded. She laughed.

"You sure do have a quick temper."

"Don't come if you don't want to."

"But I do," she protested. "I wasn't sure you wanted to."

"Then why would I ask you?" he demanded to know.

"You don't know me very well..."

"You don't know me either."

"Perhaps I do."

"What does that mean?"

"Oh - nothing - maybe I'm wrong."

"You're the first person I've been able to talk to in five years. Do you know that? For all the time I was in the hospital I never said one word to anyone. It's strange to make contact with someone just when you're at the end of the line...and someone who is lonely too and has been through it all and understands..."

From across the hall a voice was calling.

"Oh darn! Ruby's here. My cousin..."

"Tell her to wait 'til we have our drink. Don't go home yet."

"Edna! Why there you are!" Ruby made her way to them talking as she approached. Her voice was like honey bringing back long memories.

"Ruby, I'd like you to meet a friend. Oops. I don't know your name..."

"Bud Wilkerson."

"Mr Wilkerson, this is my cousin, Ruby Farmer."

"It sure is a pleasure to meet you," Ruby said.

"Ruby, would you mind waiting just a few minutes? My friend and I are going to have a drink."

"Why sure, honey. I'll meet you back here in fifteen minutes. That okay?"

"Thanks Ruby. We won't be too long." They turned to the refreshment bar.

"Two lemonades," he ordered coldly.

"You sound angry."

"Why would I be angry?"

"Maybe I could tell you, but I'd rather you told me."

"Told you what?"

"Whatever it is that's bothering you, Mr. Louisiana."

"What's Louisiana got to do with it?"

"Nothing. Everything maybe."

"Damn it to hell! All right. She sounded like a darkie! Your cousin I mean." Something wet dropped on his hand.

"My cousin Ruby is black and so am I." She turned her pale sightless eyes to his which looked blindly back.

When Ruby found her fifteen minutes later standing alone at the refreshment bar of the Social Club for the Blind, tears were falling from her sightless eyes.

Outside Bud Wilkerson stood crouched alone by the door, staring sightlessly at the cold, dark, lonely city. He felt more alone than he had ever felt. Even more alone than when he had left the hospital. As he crouched there he was fighting off the growing certainty that God or Fate or perhaps just happenstance, had finally taken pity on him and had given him his one last chance, his final crack at the can - and he had blown it.

ABSALOM

I put the phone down and stared at my desk. My wife had sobbed, "He's still not called." What can I do to console her? I say it doesn't matter, when I know it does. Sometimes I'm able to force back the pain that takes the form of a grey cloud suffusing everything, leaching life of its laughter. But then I see the sadness in my wife's eyes and I am helpless. I, who spend my time curing the illness of others, have no remedy for this. I stared out the window. The sun shone through the trees. My office was warm despite the efforts of the old air conditioner. It smelled sterile, medicinal.

My nurse knocked lightly and entered, placing on my desk the routine questionnaire that had been filled out by my last patient of the day. Glancing at my watch I said, "It's late - go home. I'll close up." Glancing at the page I noted under the question "Nature of illness" the word "Consultation."

The patient was a small man, with the straight black hair and angular features that characterize his people. He seemed to be in his late thirties, with a dignified and intelligent demeanor. His name was Nam Hua.

"What can I do for you, Mr Hua?"

He seemed to be searching for words. "I've come to ask you about the DNA test."

"Did you want one for yourself?" When he remained silent I added, "There are several forensic labs in Toronto that perform DNA tests, or I can send you to a colleague of mine, a pathologist. Do you have a time frame? Is there a special reason for this that we should know?"

The man did not speak for a few minutes, finally saying, "It's a long story. Do you have time?"

I looked at my watch and then settled back in my chair. This was the tale told to me by Nam Hua on that hot August day. He spoke in a quiet, uninflected voice that revealed none of the emotion that he must have felt. I lost track of time as he told his horrifying story.

"I studied Engineering in Montreal before the war. When I returned to Vietnam, I met Minh. She was very beautiful - a medical doctor practicing at the maternity hospital in Hue. Our parents approved of our marriage and we settled in Hue. A year later our daughter Tam was born. As I could speak French and a little English, I sometimes acted as interpreter for an American journalist during the war. Because of this, when the Americans left I was sentenced to five years in a reeducation camp. My wife could visit me only twice in all that time. The second time she brought my daughter who at four years old was afraid of me and wouldn't let me hold her. I wept when they left. I didn't know how much longer I would be imprisoned. In many cases when a prisoner's term was over, he was sentenced again to another term without any reason being given.

"But I was lucky. After five years I was released. I returned home to find that Minh had changed. The light was gone from her eyes. She had only one wish and that was to leave Vietnam. It became an obsession. One day she told me of a patient whose brother had a small boat and was willing to smuggle us to Thailand. He charged a great deal of money, but for the doctor and her family, he would charge nothing. By then there were four of us. We had a young son.

"In great secrecy, we began to make plans. We could confide in no one. Anyone - even a family member - might have betrayed us or tried to dissuade us.

"We took the children to Ho Chi Minh City for what was supposed to be a short holiday. There we waited to be contacted. In the dark of night, we boarded a bus that took us far out into the countryside. Carrying the sleeping children we walked along the beach until we found a small boat already crowded with people. Everyone spoke in whispers. You could taste and smell the fear. Even the most determined felt our bodies betray us as our limbs trembled. At three o'clock in the morning, the boat pushed off into the black water of the China Sea.

"It was hot and crowded, and the rocking of the boat and the smell of oil mixed with that of sweating, frightened people, made many passengers sick. There was no breeze. My wife had her medicine bag and helped as much as she could. No one slept very much while we were still in Vietnamese waters. Whenever a strong wave caused the boat to lurch or the sound of the engine to change, we feared we'd been caught.

"By next morning we were out of range of Vietnamese chase boats. The atmosphere changed. We brought out our food and settled on the deck to eat. Our children played with the other children, not noticing the lessened but continuing anxiety of their elders. For most of them it just seemed to be an exciting change from their everyday life. That evening as the sun went down we all breathed a sigh of relief, sure that at last we were beyond the reach of our government. Later, many people recalled what they said were bad omens. An unknown bird had flown across the sun as it fell below the horizon in a huge red ball. Someone had seen green vapour rising from the water. 'We should have known,' they said.

"We were awakened in the early dawn by terrified screaming and shouting. We found ourselves completely surrounded by a group of fishing boats. Rough looking Thai pirates armed with guns and knives were boarding our ship. They went methodically to work, robbing us of what little we'd been able to smuggle out - gold coins, pitiful jewelry.

"We pleaded with them to take what they wanted but not to harm us. They didn't understand. They spoke in a strange tongue. After searching us they ordered us to jump into the water. Those who didn't understand or showed reluctance, were pushed overboard, even children. Floundering, screaming in panic, we clung to the surrounding boats and were hauled up by the pirates still on board. In the confusion, I was separated from my wife. Minh was in terror for the children. She thrust our little boy into the arms of a woman standing near her, screaming to her to jump while Minh herself ran after our little girl Tam and leaped into the water holding her. Both women were picked up but on different boats. I could hear Minh calling out to our son.

"I don't know how we lived through that day. God must make us very strong. I try to remember that this life is transitory, that nothing has any meaning except that we give it meaning, but I couldn't control my mounting fear. With free rein, the pirates were ransacking everything, taking food and water, clothing - anything they could find. For hours they searched every part of our boat. They even dismantled and took the engine." Here Mr. Hua paused for what seemed a very long time. I hear the beat of my heart. Then with a sigh he continued.

"As morning wore on, the sun beat down on us - a small group of terrorized refugees scattered on the pirate boats. Children cried. Our son, Dao, fell asleep and the woman holding him, put him down on the deck in the shade of a sail. There, our beloved two year old boy with almond eyes just like Minh's, slept peacefully, little knowing that his whole life was being irrevocably and horribly changed."

Again Mr. Hua became silent. The clock on my desk ticked. The air conditioner whirred. Mr Hua stared at me without seeing me, and then continued, "Suddenly we heard a shout like a command from one of the pirates and we were once again roughly shoved back into the sea. Those who managed to climb back aboard our now deserted ship, held out their hands to those in the water. Minh, Tam and I were pulled aboard. But the woman who had saved our boy was thrown into the water before she could collect him. She tried to climb back onto the deck, calling out that a little boy was still aboard, but the men on the deck just pushed her back down into the sea.

"At first we didn't understand, but then in horror we heard motors starting up and saw the pirate boats beginning to move away with our little boy still aboard. I felt an iron ring around my heart. Minh, screaming,'Dao. My son, my son! Don't take my son!' leapt into the water, swimming after the departing boats. I jumped in after her and together we tried to give chase. Others on our boat pointed and screamed, trying to make them understand what was happening. The racket was fearful but the pirates didn't even look back."

Nam's whole body seemed to shake as he said these last words.

"They sailed off with our little boy."

He seemed to be reliving the entire horror of that moment. The silence was complete as though all life outside the office had stopped and there was no one left except him and me, no sound except the ticking clock and the persistent hum of the air-conditioner.

Nam continued, "When it was clearly hopeless, I tried to get Minh to turn back but she wouldn't. She fought me as though I were the enemy. If the captain had not managed to pull up alongside and haul us, still struggling, back on board, we would both have drowned. We couldn't do that. There was Tam to think about.

"Minh beseeched the captain to chase the pirates, but that was impossible without an engine and we were already in great danger so close to this area of the Thai coast.

"Minh was inconsolable, sobbing and screaming. Tam ran first to me and then to her mother in terror. I finally succeeded in coaxing Minh to take some of the tranquilizers that she had brought, and after what seemed hours the pills began to take effect. My poor wife sat numb and silent, clutching our frightened daughter.

"We drifted for days.

"According to international convention, refugees rescued in these waters became the responsibility of the government whose flag carrier rescues them. Because of this, more than one ship to which we frantically signaled, refused to stop. We were desperate, suffering dreadfully from hunger and thirst. One elderly woman died. On the fourth day, a German flagship approached and took us aboard. Minh's eyes were closed and I feared for her life.

"On the German ship we were fed and brought to a refugee camp in Singapore where we received medical treatment. We were to be processed and resettled in Germany unless we had ties to another country which would agree to take us.

"As I had studied in Montreal, I was eligible to apply for entry to Canada. That is how, sixteen years ago, we arrived in our new land. Minh bravely tried to pick up her life. She had become a doctor in Vietnam because she wanted to help others. But in Canada, although she passed the requisite tests, she was unable to get the internship she needed in order to receive accreditation to practice medicine. After several years of knocking on every door, she gave up. She lived without dreams. I found a job as an Engineer with a small auto parts company and was able to save a little money.

"When the political situation eased in Vietnam, Minh flew to Thailand to seek our son. For years we had been sending money to a group of monks - money to pay for notices to be placed in coastal villages. Surely someone must have seen a small Vietnamese boy growing up in a Thai village. Or perhaps our son himself - if he were still alive - now old enough to read such a notice, would dimly recall being plucked from the water. But Minh's search was fruitless. The monks proved false. They had taken our money but had posted few notices. And the refugee organizations turned up nothing. After several months Minh returned home to Tam and me, ill and depressed.

"More years passed. And suddenly, there was news. It came about in a strange and unanticipated way. A monk in Ho Chi Minh city had gotten into a conversation with a young cyclo driver, intrigued because the boy, who was obviously Vietnamese, spoke with the accent of a foreigner. When asked about it, the boy shrugged and said he was an orphan who had grown up in Thailand. After being treated badly there, he'd managed to swim across the Mekong into Vietnam.

"The monk remembered hearing somewhere of a child kidnapped by Thai pirates. He took the boy's name and address and notified one of the refugee organizations which recently got in touch with me in Canada."

I leaned forward, "There is hope then?"

He didn't address my question directly as he replied, "I've said nothing to my wife. She's been through too much. If this is a false alarm, I don't want the wound reopened. And this boy, even if he is our son, what would he be like now? Cyclo drivers are notorious in Ho Chi Minh City. They are the dregs of society, often forced by their syndicates to pimp, steal, sell drugs.

"I asked a friend, a lawyer in the city, to approach the boy and under some pretext find out more about him. Xuan found the boy and discovered that his earliest memories were of a small village in Thailand. His 'mother' had been a sickly village woman who was taunted by the others for taking care of the 'fish' as they called him. He was found in the water they said, and should be thrown back.

The woman protected him as best she could. He was used as a slave by the fishermen who made him do heavy physical work from the time he was able to lift and pull.

"When he was still young - he had no idea how old he actually was - the woman died and he ran away, making his way eventually to Bangkok where he lived by his wits, and finally, when he realized that he was Vietnamese, he had come to Vietnam. His language was coarse, his behavior the same. If there was any nobility in his soul, it was not evident to Xuan.

"But the events surrounding the boy's sudden appearance, and his apparent age, make it possible that he's our son and I want to know. I can't get a blood sample from him without explaining the situation and I don't want to raise any false hopes in the boy. Is there another way? Hair or finger nails - it might not be easy but maybe Xuan could ..." His voice trailed off.

"Does the boy smoke?" I asked.

"Everyone in Vietnam smokes. I'm sure he does."

"Then tell your friend to collect some of the cigarette stubs for analysis. It's a rather complicated process, a matter of matching patterns, but it can be done. Am I correct in assuming that you will want the pathologist to compare a sample of your DNA with his?"

Nam Hoa's head barely nodded.

"If you have no objection, then, I would like to turn this over to Dr. Hollen, the pathologist I spoke of. When you have the cigarette butts - it's the saliva on the butts that will be analyzed - call him for an appointment. At that time, he'll probably take a sample of your blood."

"Does it take very long? What must they do?"

"Depends on how busy he is, but it does take some time. DNA might be described as a ruler with notches on it. Scientists select certain notches on the ruler - that is, sections of the DNA chain - of one sample, and compare them to another to see to what extent they match. Except in identical twins, no two will ever match exactly, but between close relatives, there are a certain predictable number of matches. Forensic scientists develop sections of the DNA, or markers - for comparison. The samples are then applied to a blank strip of chemically treated paper or film and developed. It's a cumbersome process and may take a few months. But we can tell today, with what we call mathematical certainty, whether two people are related. Dr. Hollen will be able to tell you exactly how long it will take."

I stood up, and as I ushered Mr. Hoa out I said, "We ought to be able to tell you whether this boy is indeed your son."

The look that he turned on me then was to haunt me, so suffused was it with longing and anguish. When I closed the door behind him I sat at my desk for a long time lost in thought.

More than two years were to pass before I saw Nam Hoa again, and then it was a chance encounter in a small Vietnamese restaurant. I was already seated when I saw him come past accompanied by a handsome woman I felt sure was Minh, and a young couple carrying a baby. I hailed him. He stopped, looking puzzled. He didn't recognize me until I mentioned my name. Then, glancing anxiously at his family which stood expectantly around him, he introduced his wife, his daughter Tam and her husband. Noting his embarrassment, I quickly said, "I don't wonder that you didn't recognize me. I met you in connection with your work - engineering, isn't it? I have a photographic memory for faces and am always doing this to people. Sorry."

His tension evaporated as the questioning look left Minh's face. Before they walked on, I said, "Give me a call. I'd love to hear from you." He nodded and the little family moved on to their table. Looking behind me, I saw Minh taking off her grandson's snow suit and settling him into a high chair while she hugged and kissed him.

Two weeks later Nam Hoa came to see me. "I am ashamed that I didn't come back..." he began.

"Not at all," I assured him. "Everything you told me was confidential and you are under no obligation to tell me more unless you want to."

"I'll tell you now."

"You understand..."

"I know I don't have to. But I would like to."

With great dignity, Nam Hoa continued his story. His sentences were clipped. Often he fell into deep silences before continuing. Outside my window, snow was falling noiselessly.

"I took the cigarette stubs, sent me by my friend, to your colleague, the pathologist. He took a sample of my blood. The very next day I left for Vietnam. I went alone. I told Minh I was going to visit my father who is old now and ailing. In Ho Chi Minh City, I went to meet the boy."

Nam Hoa fell silent. "I returned home after a week."

"Did you go back to Dr. Hollen?"

"I did."

He said nothing more. Torn by curiosity, I prodded him . "Did he have the results of the test?"

"He said that he was almost 100% sure, but he wanted to be certain. He asked me to return in a week. The suspense was unbearable, but it gave me a great deal of time to think."

"And when you went back," I found myself asking anxiously, "what was the result?"

Nam Hoa did not answer directly. But as though in a dream, he said, "I met the 'fish' in Ho Chi Minh City. It was a strange sensation. I searched his face to see if there was any family resemblance - perhaps there was, I wasn't sure. There was something in his appearance, perhaps it was the eyes... but his manners were those of the streets - tough, coarse and rude. He had no education, no regard for anything except enough money for his next smoke." He smiled ruefully.

"I asked him to take me around the city and kept talking to him, trying to find a clue. Always he demanded more than the price agreed upon. This, you see, is what they do - especially to visitors from overseas. They think those who emigrated are rich. I suppose in comparison to them, we are. And why did I expect him to be different? It's unpleasant, but for them it's a matter of survival."

"I understand," I said to reassure him though with sinking heart. What hornet's nest had this desperate father stirred up? Was the boy with them? Had they brought him to Canada, or found out to their ambivalent relief that he was not their son?

"At my urging, the 'fish' - everyone called him that still - took me to where he slept - an abandoned warehouse, a single storey shed with dirt floors - that he shared with several filthy looking men. There was nowhere to wash, no way to keep clean, and the place was strewn with unspeakable things. I questioned him to see if he had any memories going back beyond his stay in the Thai fishing village. He had none though he showed me scars on his back from the beatings he'd received in the village. One day I told him how we escaped, leaving out the loss of our son. He wasn't interested. Sometimes I wanted to tell him everything, and at other times I was repelled by him. I decided that the doctor's report would decide his fate - and ours."

Nam Hoa fell silent. I was about to question him when he asked quietly, "Doctor, in English is there a difference in the meaning of the words 'son' and 'offspring'? Isn't one a larger concept rather than simply a genetic fact? Is there a deeper meaning to the word, 'son'? Isn't a son someone who shares your values, your memories, your love, even though he may not share your genes? Isn't a son someone with whom you have bonded over years of shared experience?"

I found myself unaccountably anxious. My heart was pounding, and sweat broke out on my forehead. I was accustomed to giving authoritative answers to those who came seeking solace or understanding, but I found I had no answers to Nam Hoa's tortured questions. I had to face my own pain suddenly and sharply. I had to face my own relationship with my son. It had proved a profound disappointment to my wife and me, but how was that relevant? There was no question that he was our biological son....or offspring. He and I had a lifetime of shared experiences. And yet....what was it that constituted a son? Was it simply a biological fact? The word 'son' held so much poignancy for me, such unsatisfied longing.

As though reading my thoughts, Nam Hoa continued, "Look at the animal world. In most species, as soon as a pup or a cub is grown, it's no longer recognized by its mother. Why do we human beings feel that parenthood is forever? What obligations does the relationship place on parents - and on their children - and for how long? What do they owe each other? Has society ever codified this?"

I sat in silence my heart racing as he continued, "I asked myself, do I have an obligation to this young man -if he is indeed our son - to save him from his terrible life? And what if he's not our son, does that obligation disappear? Are they not all our sons in some sense?"

He looked tortured - too much in his own bubble of anguish to note the perspiration on my brow, as he continued, "And what of my obligation to the saved, to my wife and daughter? They have finally come to terms with the loss of a son and brother. If we took this young stranger in and it didn't work out, what would it do to them? We would lose a son for a second time. Over the years, they have - we all have - built him into a mythical figure, someone who will make up for all the suffering we've gone through. He could never live up to such expectations. And we could never make up to him for the suffering that he has had. Could he ever forgive us? Could we ever forgive him?"

I thought of my own son, living in Vancouver, rarely if ever showing concern for his parents or his sisters - a son who could not even remember his mother's sixtieth birthday. Perhaps animals had the right idea. Still, many years ago in those early glory days, when we were young, my son and I were best of friends. We sailed together. We camped out together. I could see myself reflected in his eyes as a heroic figure, I never dreamed it would turn out the way it has. Now he is estranged, angry, sarcastic and contemptuous of his parents' way of life. What terrible thing did we do to him, always with the best of intentions? Why has it gone so terribly wrong?

We both sat silently, adrift in our own formless agony, and then, leaning toward Nam Hoa, I asked, or rather stated, "So you decided..."

"Yes."

When Nam Hoa left, it was a long time before I summoned my next patient. At the end of the day, I picked up the phone and dialed Dr. Hollen's number. But before anyone could answer, I hung up.

THE MONEY ORDER

When the doorbell rang, Joanne still had the letter in her hand. She smiled at the rumpled young man standing at the door. Richard was the top fashion photographer of New York City, welcomed in the homes of the rich and famous. His photographs celebrated their status in every issue of *Vogue*, *Harpers Bazaar* and *Town and Country*. And he dressed the part. On a freezing December day, a few weeks before Christmas, he was wearing blue jeans, a dark blue, hand-tailored shirt under a heavy off-white sweater, a light windbreaker and a knitted stocking cap, no gloves, and on his feet a pair of dirty white sneakers.

"Aren't you freezing?" she asked as she led him in.

"I'm used to it," he said. Later over a steaming cup of hot cocoa he asked, "What's the matter? You're not yourself today."

"It's nothing really," she started, and then pointed helplessly at the letter now lying on the coffee table. "I received this just this morning, and I don't know what to do about it."

He picked up the letter. The date on it was a few weeks old, November 1965. It read:

URGENT APPEAL! A group of five high school protesters, followers of Dr Martin Luther King, were arrested yesterday in McComb, Mississippi, during a peaceful demonstration against state segregation laws. The charges against them will not hold up in any court of law, but local authorities are determined to keep these young people jailed through Christmas.

Bail has been set deliberately high as the authorities are well aware that these youngsters and their families have no financial resources. In order to secure the release of these young people in time for them to spend Christmas with their families, we need to raise $14,000 bail by December 23.

"Time is so short. Can you help?"

He read no further."When did you get this?" he asked.

"This morning. A friend forwarded it to me in hopes that I could do something, but it's too late. I feel helpless." Joanne looked distraught. "These are just a bunch of idealistic teenagers. I can't bear the thought of them in jail - and for Christmas!"

He pursed his lips and his eyebrows came together in a scowl.

"Can I keep the letter?" he asked. "I've got a lot of clients who owe me — clients able to help and who might want to."

"You have only a few days," Joanne said doubtfully. "How can you raise the money and get it to them in time? You can't send a check, it would never clear in time! You'd have to send a money order and you've only a week! If the money isn't mailed by Friday it'll never get there in time. No, it's hopeless!"

"Can I have the letter?" he asked.

"Of course, take it. Do what you can, but...." her words trailed off.

During the next few days the photographer ran about the city non-stop. He called on famous actresses, society belles, editors of fashion magazines. He sat in sumptuous living rooms, on Louis XIV chairs covered in glazed chintzes surrounded by magnificent collections of Chinese artifacts and Japanese netsuke. He called on best selling writers in funky Soho lofts, dominated by huge Jackson Pollack paintings. He called on media barons in wood paneled dens surrounded by Mogdiglianis and Renoirs, on captains of industry, perched on Mies Van der Rohe chairs covered in buttery leather with mammoth Frank Stella or de Kooning paintings on the wall. Everywhere he went he took the crumpled letter out of his pocket. Whenever he left it was with a sizable check in his hand.

In the late afternoon of Friday, December 17, he picked up the last check. If he got the money in the mail that day, the kids could be out by Christmas!

It was getting dark and snow was beginning to fall as he darted through heavy traffic, racing to get to the post office before it closed. A previous call had assured him that the money order window was open until five-thirty.

He dodged through heavy crowds of New Yorkers who were scurrying about buying last minute gifts for the holiday. The arctic air smelled clean and clear. An icy wind kept the traffic fumes at bay. Although the cold was frigid, cutting right through his sweater and light windbreaker, he could feel perspiration trickling down his sides. He was anxious, lest time run out. In his nervous haste, he ran into people and hastily apologized. Glancing at his watch, he noted that it was just after five as he dashed up the slippery steps of the imposing Post Office at 33rd Street and Ninth Avenue. He felt elated. He had made it!

Snow was falling lightly from a dark steel grey sky as he entered the huge building. The place smelled of warm wet wool. He stamped his feet, glad to be out of the cold. Ancient radiators hissed and reluctantly released warm air into the cavernous space. He looked about for the Money Order window and his heart fell. Beads of sweat formed on his forehead. The window was barred and completely dark. The ajacent windows were closed as well, and there was no one at the main counter. Far in the back, under a single hanging bulb, a young man with a wispy blond beard, was sorting mail.

"Hey!" the photographer called. "Where's the guy whose supposed to be handling money orders?"

"Gone home."

"But I called - he's supposed to be here for another half hour!"

"Yeah man, but it started snowing and he had to get home to Long Island. Come again on Monday."

"Can you get him back here?"

"Are you kidding? I told you, he lives on Long Island."

"Can you help me with a money order?"

"Nah, that's his department. I can't do it."

The photographer stood staring into the darkened recesses of the Post Office. All his efforts of the last few days had been for nothing. The promises he had made to himself and to all the others, had been broken. He had lost the fight. If he had been able to come just a half hour earlier.... He was not used to failing and it hurt. He couldn't bear the thought of the kids in prison. He turned to leave. He didn't hear the lone postal worker come forward to the counter until he heard him say, "Sorry. I'd help you if I could. But I can't do money orders."

He was a tall lean young man, his blond hair tied neatly in back. The photographer turned around, looked at him intently, then started to go again. Then on impulse, he turned to face him and said quietly, "Have you ever heard of McComb, Mississippi?"

"Can't say that I have."

"I'd like to tell you about some kids in McComb," the photographer began. When he had finished his story, the young postal worker stared at him for a moment and then reached for the telephone and dialed the number of his colleague in Long Island.

"Hi, Marla. Let me speak to Pete," he said. "Hey Pete! This is Joe. No, no trouble, everything's okay. I was just wonderin' - have you ever heard of McComb, Mississippi? See, there's a bunch of kids down there...."

When Joe put down the phone, he pointed to the bench and said, "Sit down. He's coming back."

It was a long wait. The skies were black and the snow coming down hard when Pete arrived. He was a gray-haired black man, with a bit of a paunch and deep lines under his eyes. The photographer felt a stab of compunction at having brought him away from the warmth of his home on such an evening so close to Christmas, but then remembered that it was not his choice. Pete had decided to come back.

The kids were out of jail in time to go to church on Christmas Eve. They thought it was a miracle. And it was a miracle. A miracle wrought by people far away who cared enough to create a miracle.

THE SOOEY PILL

It was the pill society. There was the morning-after pill of course, which the government had made obligatory, after the first child. Yet even so, the population growth was alarming, and overcrowding was becoming desperate. Then there were the multitude of tranquilizer pills in almost every color, size and shape that helped one to cope with the tensions caused by the almost total lack of privacy, by the constant noise, the polluted air, continual abrasive physical contact with crowds, and by the harsh and ugly sights of a super industrialization, devoid of trees or greenery of any kind.

Then there were the food pills. One took them three times a day. The endless wheat fields, pastures, grazing lands and vegetable farms of former days had become ancient history. Even the Grand Canyon was now filled to overflowing with sweating humanity, jostling endlessly for living space. The food pills were processed in huge floating factories and consisted of compressed algae, seaweed and plankton. They had an unpleasant fishy taste, but could be swallowed whole with a glass of desalinated water, and they provided all the nutriments necessary to go on living.

But the most important pill of all was affectionately called the Sooey pill. It was the only one that came in a lavender color with a stamp on it resembling a clenched fist. Every person was issued one of these on his or her twenty-first birthday. If one lost the Sooey, another could be issued - but only after much red tape; and of course, one's name was permanently placed on a "Suspects List," to be consulted every time someone was murdered by misuse of the Sooey. These suspects automatically came under police surveillance and were questioned at great length, and if one's Sooey disappeared, one knew oneself to be at best a possible unwitting accessory to murder. For this reason, and others, people took great care not to lose their Sooeys.

Basically the entire society was built around the Sooey pill. It was not only the individual's escape hatch, but society depended on it, as a regulator in a world where nature's own regulators seemed to have fused out, or gone haywire. There had been much talk - and the Radical Demopubs had actually tried to force through, a bill to issue the Sooey pill at age thirteen or younger - with the motive of issuing the pill before childbearing age. It was a desperate measure, attempting to deal with a desperate situation. But the Demopubs were overruled by the conservative wing of their own party, which joined with the opposition in saying that it was an inhuman solution, and that the situation was not yet that desperate - an indication in itself, some people muttered - of things to come.

But perhaps it would not become necessary ever to pass that bill, as living conditions were indeed fast becoming so intolerable that the Sooey, or suicide pill, was being used with ever-increasing frequency. People rarely reached forty before using it, and then desisted only because of an excessive love for their child and a desire, more sentimental than reasoned, to help the child reach adulthood. Parents who felt less responsible or loving were using the Sooey in greater and greater numbers - in their thirties, when the child was likely to be a teenager, or even younger. This was a great help to the government despite the large number of orphans.

But the government did not of course sanction murder as a solution, as this would have opened the gates to total chaos and anarchy. Therefore, when thirteen year old Billy Overton was found dead of Sooey poisoning, the police went to work as they always did - to seek the perpetrator of this heinous deed. The boy had been a happy, healthy, loving child, and his parents were beside themselves with grief.

The "Suspects List" was immediately consulted and the computer was put to work. It came up with only three names - all people who had lost their Sooey, of course, and who, in addition had somehow been near the scene of the crime or had known the murdered boy. All three seemed most unlikely suspects, but the police were determined to track down every clue.

One was a taxi driver, who had lost his Sooey some eight weeks ago, and whose only connection with Billy was that he had dropped off a passenger three blocks from the Overton apartment an hour or so before the crime was committed. As it would have taken him about that long to drive the three blocks to the Overtons, he became a prime suspect. But the fact remained that he insisted he had never laid eyes on Billy and all objective evidence seemed to bear out his contention. And what possible motive could he have?

The second suspect turned up by the computer was a woman who lived within walking distance of the Overtons, had lost her Sooey pill three months before, and was just about to have a new one reissued. She knew the Overtons vaguely, but never remembered having met Billy, although she may have passed him many times on the busy, frantically overcrowded street; and surely, she insisted, she had no wish to kill the young boy. She was married but as yet had no child of her own. And what possible motive could she have? She was known to be a quiet almost apathetic type.

The third suspect seemed even more remote than the other two. The computer turned up the name of Bobby's first grade teacher who had lost her Sooey three days previous to the murder; but she now lived three hundred miles away. Since any type of transport had to be reserved months in advance, she couldn't possibly have been at the scene of the murder even in the highly unlikely situation that she had somehow conceived a hatred for Billy in first grade and, harboring this dislike, had resolved seven years later to kill him! It was utter nonsense and the police knew it. But Billy was dead and someone had killed him.

Inspector Fenner was nearing forty-two and only his deep attachment to his sixteen-year old daughter kept him from using his own Sooey. His wife had used hers the year before, after writing him a heartbreaking farewell note begging forgiveness for leaving him to bring up their Hannah but she could bear the stifling tension no longer. Inspector Fenner had held her in his arms as she gratefully breathed her last, so he knew the suffering of the bereaved.

He now regarded the Overtons with great compassion. Billy's father, while obviously grief-stricken, was tying to console his wife, but she was beyond consolation. Her eyes were red-rimmed and swollen, with dark black circles underneath. She sobbed continually in great gasping tearless sobs.

"Billy is better off, my darling," her husband told her. "You know that. How often have we spoken of the horrors of this world, of the horrors that awaited him - horrors that would envelope our Billy more and more as he grew older and came to realize what the world is like. You, who never wanted him to stop smiling. You, who protected him and built an imaginary world around him - you must know and be grateful that he is released now from the ghastly, grey, grim, unrelieved life that we live."

Inspector Fenner could bear no more. He left the parents to their inconsolable grief. But the call to duty was too strong, too deeply ingrained in him. He returned the next day and in the gentlest of voices asked the Overtons to show him their Sooey pills.

"What!" said Billy's father, in anger. He was afraid the police officer wanted to take them away. Reassured, he brought forth his precious little lavender pill with the clenched fist stamped on it. Mrs. Overton just stood staring at the Inspector.

Three months later, after the trial, Inspector Fenner leaned over his sleeping Hannah, slumbering among hundreds of others in the unmarried women's dormitory of their apartment complex, and kissed her good-bye. That night he gratefully used his own Sooey pill, unable to bear the reverberating screams that kept resounding in his ears - screams that he had heard that afternoon -screams of Mrs. Overton after the sentencing.

Until his last breath he heard her shrieking dementedly to the court, "Have mercy! Have mercy! I did it to save him, I loved him so dearly! Don't make me live! For God's sake, don't make me live!"

But the Court refused to reissue her Sooey.

THE FUNERAL

The few mourners fidgeted nervously on dark wood benches, trying to keep their gaze from the open coffin placed in front of them. On either side stood an urn filled with red flowers in stark contrast to the dark wood walls, bare of ornament. Organ music was piped in from speakers at either side of the chapel. There was no natural light, only that thrown by yellow bulbs set in several chandeliers. Outside it was snowing, a wet snow that turned quickly into slush and melted into the garbage and refuse underfoot on the city streets. Inside the chapel it was warm - too warm.

In the front rows sat members of the family waiting impatiently for the rabbi to appear. They did not have long to wait. Within a few minutes, a portly, serious man, wearing heavy glasses stepped forward on the dais. Adjusting his prayer shawl, he began to read from the prayer book. He motioned for the mourners to rise and join him in reciting the ancient hypnotically rhythmic Hebrew prayer for the dead, "Yisgadal, v'yisgadosh..." The scattered mourners, many of them elderly, struggled to their feet. The shrunken widow was helped by her son, who steadied her as she forced herself to stand erect. He held tightly to one of her pencil-thin arms. Her face was expressionless.

After the prayer the mourners sat down with a collective sigh, benches creaking under their shifting weight as the rabbi began to talk about the deceased.

"He was a good man. A quiet man...."

Suddenly a querulous voice was heard. Above the words of the rabbi, above the rustling and coughing of the mourners, the voice echoed loud and insistent.

"I have to go to the bathroom."

"Shh..." someone said.

Startled, the mourners at first did not know where the voice had come from. They looked about them fearing an interloper. In the silence, they heard a hushed whisper, "Can't you wait, Mother?" Somewhere someone giggled nervously.

"I cannot wait. I am in pain. I must go to the bathroom." The voice was more insistent now.

The mourners located the voice. It came from the widow, thin, grey-haired, her lips set sternly in defiance of all that life had meted out to her, including this latest indignity.

There was a hurried whispering and then two granddaughters came forward to help their grandmother to her feet. They led her shuffling up the long aisle, supporting her as she slowly, slowly put one foot ahead of the other. Her heavy wrinkled stockings collapsed into shoes too large for her feet. She moved in slow motion as though walking on ice, every step dangerous. The mourners watched, hypnotized.

When she reached the door of the chapel the rabbi, lifting his glasses onto his forehead, peered into the front rows. Addressing the eldest sister he asked, "Shall I go on or would you like me to wait?"

The son replied, "We should wait." The rabbi nodded in agreement and seated himself in a chair at the back of the bema. The mourners settled back in their seats.

The eldest daughter turned to the people seated just behind her, "So!" she said. "I hear there's going to be a wedding!"

The atmosphere changed instantly. The women began talking animatedly. The din grew louder as the upcoming wedding was discussed in every detail. Bridal outfits were described, hairdos commented upon, recipes exchanged. The men too, enjoying the brief relaxation of tension, began to talk among themselves about the stock market, business news, their prostate problems.

It seemed rather an interruption, an intrusion, when the old lady, still flanked by her two young helpers, shuffled slowly back into the sanctuary. She looked neither left nor right, but stared straight ahead as she made her way slowly to her seat. Her son rose to help her as her granddaughters returned to find their places. His mother did not look at him or acknowledge his help. Wrapped in a cocoon of bitterness, she lowered her shriveled, wizened body onto the hard bench. Her lips compressed, her face expressionless, she was a pillar of defiance - defiance against life - defiance against God.

People were reluctantly recovering their former solemnity amidst a chorus of "Sh.." and "Shush," and "Shush yourself!" The rabbi rose, adjusting his spectacles as he took his former place at the lectern and began once again to read from the prayer book. The son did not follow the words. He was trying to imagine the stony woman beside him as a young bride. He knew from older family members that she had once been a vivacious young woman, bright and ambitious. But all that was gone by the time he was born, thirteen years after his next eldest sister. He had never seen her smile. She had never kissed him. She did what she had to do to keep him clean and fed - no more, no less. She never hit him, she never hugged him.

She had worked as a secretary for a theatrical firm when she was a young girl and had fallen in love with a songwriter. They were head over heels in love and then came the stock market crash. The song writer could not find work, and her father had forbidden the match. What prospects were there for a song writer during the Great Depression? The son supposed his grandfather felt he was acting responsibly toward his daughter, but she stopped living after that. Brought up in a deeply religious family, it was unthinkable that she should flout her father's wishes. After a tearful farewell, she never saw the song writer again. He left the city. Years later she heard he had married. Two years after his marriage he had died suddenly.

His grandfather brought home a young man from the fur factory in which he worked. This was the man for his daughter, he said. The young worker had just arrived from Europe and spoke English poorly. He gave off an odor from the dead animal skins that he had to work on all day. But he had a job and was attracted to the young woman, and flattered by the older man's choice of him, a new immigrant, for a son-in-law. It was decided then between the two men - the father and the worker - that there was to be a wedding. The bride-to-be and her mother had nothing to say.

The son wondered if his mother had ever smiled again. Certainly he had never seen her smile. She had given birth to three children. Two daughters and then much later, an unwanted, unplanned son. He tried to imagine his mother in the act of love but his imagination failed him. How could this woman who never smiled, fold into a loving embrace? It was not possible.

His mother never reconciled herself to her husband - his father - a simple, gentle man. She cooked his meals and she ironed his clothes, but she was not obliged to love him and she did not - she would not. What little love she had to give she had given to his sisters and that meager store had completely dried up by the time her son was born. He wondered if, when his sisters were young, she had smiled at them or had given them the occasional furtive hug when no one was about? Certainly his sisters loved their mother and always sided with her. They saw their father through her eyes, as weak and ineffectual. Their mother was their bastion of strength.

He imagined nurses in the hospital where he was born handing him to his mother - a tiny bundle wrapped in a blanket. What had she done? She must have handed him back without comment. When he was a young boy, returning home from school, hungry and full of animal spirits, she would send him to his childless aunt, his father's sister, who lived upstairs. It was this aunt who gave the boy the only maternal love and warmth that he knew.

His father loved him, he knew that, but this wearied man was dessicate and despairing by the time the boy was born. He could tell that his father loved him by the way he reached out to him, placing his hand occasionally on the young boy's head, or on his shoulder. These shows of affection were the more precious for being random and rare, always accompanied by a reticence as if fearful of rejection. In an altercation, his father did not dare to stand up for the boy, but his look of sympathy and support made him a secret if ineffectual accomplice. For too long the boy's father had tried to win his wife's regard. In failure, he blamed himself. He lost his sense of self-worth. He became a worn husk of a man who almost never spoke. When he put on his shabby overcoat in the mornings, his wife never looked up. He rode the crowded subways to and from work, stumbling home exhausted in the evening always with that slight odor of dead animals clinging to his skin and hair. During his entire life, he had worked at the same fur factory. He was a loyal and valued employee who got incremental raises over the decades, but never a promotion.

Now in his coffin, the old man lay grey, emaciated and impassive. To his son he appeared - not happy - he had never been happy since the day of his wedding - but satisfied somehow. The expression on his face, the compression of his colorless lips, his deeply lined face and closed eyes, indicated clearly that here, at the end, his bleak view of life had been vindicated. And now death had turned out to be not so different from life after all, only quieter. More peaceful. Nothing really.

ON GROWING OLD

What is the worst thing about growing old, you ask? Growing old's not really so bad. It's even comfortable in a lot of ways, but the worst thing, really the most frustrating thing, is that your hearing turns fuzzy and sound gets lost, and with it goes much of your understanding of what is going on around you. You can no longer hear the idle comment on the bus that you were not meant to hear, can no longer catch a remark made at the other end of the table, can no longer even hear the whispered comment that you definitely were meant to hear. Perhaps I'm at a party and my husband whispers, "Let's get out of here, it's so boring."

In front of everyone, I reply, "What? What's boring?"

Or - this happened to me the other day. A friend asked, "What are you planning to serve at your dinner party?"

I answered, "Veal chops." The only thing was, she didn't ask me what I was serving, she asked me what I was wearing.

I'm not really deaf. It's just that all the sounds are astigmatic - if I can mix my senses a bit. Nothing is crystal clear anymore. An important part of your life has disappeared, cut away, amputated. When you're dining out and the two people at the next table are having what is evidently a juicy argument, you see their heated gestures, their angry red faces, but you can't hear - oh, maybe a word now and then - but only enough to tantalize, to make you wild to know what it's all about. When listening to TV, in order to get the fuzziness out a bit, you have to turn the volume so high that your neighbors down the street don't bother switching on their sound to listen to the evening news or *Masterpiece Theater*. The most heavily overused word in my vocabulary these days is, "What?"

I keep turning to my husband to ask, "What did he say?" only to have him shrug his shoulders. We are two peas in a sound-proofed pod.

It's funny about the senses - so many have double meanings, and

142

often these secondary qualities get better with age. We all have an inner voice, a sort of alter ego, that expresses our conscience, our best self. I try to listen to that voice. But it's not always omniscient. I wish it was.

They say that with age all of our five senses begin to give out. But I've had two cataract operations and my eyes are so good that I don't need glasses anymore. People a lot younger than me wear glasses - I notice you are. So that's one of my senses that's doing just fine.

And the sense of sight or vision goes beyond what the eye can see and becomes heightened by years of experience. Sometimes you feel you can see right into people. As you get older you seem to gain in that sixth sense called insight or intuition.

Smell? You're supposed to lose your sense of smell too as the years go by. That's probably true because my husband who had a sense of smell like a bloodhound when we were young - he used to walk into a room and say, "What died in here?"- doesn't say that as much any more, although the other day he said our bedroom smells like dog piss. I don't smell it, and that's just fine with me. I think he's exaggerating, though to show me that he's as good as he ever was - and in some respects I have to admit he is. But we won't go into that. And it's a certainty that our dog, grown old along with us, has abandoned all attempts at being house trained as though he can't be bothered at his age. I know the feeling.

The sense of smell has sort of a double meaning. You smell a rat. And maybe as the physical sense diminishes, your intuition fills the gap. You sure can smell trouble .

Let's see. There's the sense of touch or feel. Mine is fine as far as I can tell.

But feeling means more than simply reaching out to touch something. You can touch people in many ways, and you feel things in many ways as well. But I'll tell you a secret. I'm shutting down on my feelings a little bit these days. Oh, it's not that I don't love. I love as passionately as I ever did. But those who hurt me or who have the potential to hurt me, I keep at bay. I'm determined not to be as vulnerable as I once was because it's harder now to shrug it off. I have no time to be hurt anymore. I'm talking about one's children, of course, as many of you - those of you who are older - have probably guessed.

They say that all children disappoint their parents - or is it that all parents are disappointed in their children? It doesn't quite mean the same thing. Some children seem to grow up to be so different from their parents and sometimes even from their siblings, with unfamiliar ways of doing things and a seeming lack of love and respect for their parents. Perhaps people should just let go of the feelings that tie you together when you oughtn't to be together at all. And after a while you get to thinking, "You're a long time dead," so who cares really? You try to get beyond the surprise and the hurt. Anyway, things don't seem as cataclysmic as they once did. That's what I mean by shutting down the feelings a little bit. If you care all the time, you're going to be going around like the walking wounded. When you're young there are many distractions to help you forget. It's different when you're older - you can't throw things off the way you used to. That's why I'm trying to learn how to grow a crust around my feelings a little bit.

It's a strange thing but while in some ways I am more impatient with things - stupidity or a lack of kindness, at the same time I seem to be feeling more forgiving, less intolerant these days. That's odd because they say as you get older you get more testy. I haven't. There's still so much to know, and less time in which to get to know it. Most of all I'm curious about people. Why they are the way they are. When I was young, I was much quicker to judge. Now I appreciate differences. I don't judge those kids who wear their hair in blue and green spikes and have rings in their tongues. I'm sure many of them are really nice kids - just a little screwed up maybe. They'll grow out of it. Still, I suppose I wouldn't be glad if one of them was a grandkid of mine. I haven't gotten that tolerant.

Oh, there are still some areas in which I'm as intolerant as ever. Take politics for instance - but then, if I like people, sometimes I just steer clear of politics so I don't have to rearrange my attitude about them. It's all so meaningless anyway - politics, I mean. The politicians do what they want and for their own reasons regardless of how we feel about it.

Finally there's the fifth sense - the sense of taste. I still love good food even though it often doesn't agree with me. I used to be able to eat a huge meal and enjoy every course. Now I look at a plate laden with food as a potential minefield. Of course, a lot of that comes from the fact that when we were young, food was supposed to be good for you. Now it's all proven to be poison. I heard a lecture the other day in which the speaker said that meat is loaded with hydrogenated fats, processed foods have transfatty acids, dairy products were never intended to be consumed after childhood, gluten products are so altered that they're almost impossible to digest and sugar is empty calories. I left the lecture trying to think of what was left. Rice and steamed vegetables? Now we hear that these too - along with everything else - have been genetically altered. Non-genetically altered, organic fruit is probably okay if it didn't look so mealy. But fruit, we are told, is never to be eaten with protein as it will ferment in your stomach causing bloating and flatulence. Oops. There's another rather unpleasant age-related symptom. I often hesitate to enter an elevator these days if someone else is already there.

Apart from the dinner table, taste has a multitude of meanings. In fact the dictionary lists about ten. "To experience for the first time" - such as the taste of freedom - or of old age. Or "the distinguishing flavour of something" such as the taste of a summer rain, for instance - or of old age.

I won't go into all of them, but of course there is the one that is defined thus "the ability to notice, appreciate and judge what is beautiful." I think I have that. But tastes change, don't they? Taste in music for instance. Would you believe that I don't know a single modern pop song - and don't want to? A screecher - they're all screechers to me - may have sold millions around the world, and their songs may be playing in the background of every supermarket or department store I enter, but I don't hear them. And that's not because my hearing is so bad, it's because I tune them out. To be honest, I don't know how I do that. I can't tune out those irritating background sounds on television, whether music or traffic or whatever the director has decided to put in to heighten verisimilitude and ensure that hearing the dialogue is impossible.

How did I get started on all this? Oh yes, the worst thing about getting old. As I say, the worst thing is, in a sense, not being able to eavesdrop on the world around you. Does this surprise you? I'm sure it's not quite what you expected. You probably expected me to talk about creaky and achy joints, leaky bladder or age spots. I have all those things but they don't get in my way too much. Perhaps you expected me to talk about the loss of intellectual powers. Well, it's true that every morning I find millions of brain cells lying on my pillow. I try to scoop them up but I know I'm losing them all the time. Still, the experts tell us that we start losing them in our twenties if not sooner, but that there are so many billions of them it's scarcely noticeable. I do notice, of course, but mostly when it comes to forgetting things like your name - which isn't that important. Sorry! Of course your name is important to you, but not so much to me - I guess you can understand that. I mean I can always ask you your name and there it is. It isn't like it's permanently forgotten and consigned to the ash heap. There are other things that I've forgotten though, things that now that my parents and others in the preceding generations are gone, can never be retrieved. I truly mourn the loss of those memories. But then I remember that they would die with me anyway, so what's the difference?

Where was I? Oh yes, that's another thing. Forgetting what you were talking about. But we all do that. Even my daughter does that sometimes, and I have to remind her. A friend told me that she went to the refrigerator, opened the door and stood there, unable to remember what she had gone there for. Finally, her husband called out, "Why don't you just climb in and shut the door so the food won't spoil?"

Yes, I'm losing brain cells all the time, but so are you very likely and it's just a matter of how far along on the moving belt we are. I'm pretty far along but I don't see the end yet, and I'm glad of that. And I have my faculties, as they say, so that isn't a real problem.

What? Speak up! I didn't hear what you said! I think as long as I can say, "Speak Up!" I will be truly alive. But I can see a point when

I will be tired of saying, "What?" or perhaps of people shouting at me when all it takes is a slightly elevated and clear voice. Then I will sink back, as I do sometimes even now, and simply remain unaware of what is being said around me or even to me. Hearing doesn't get better - only worse. How awful it will be if one day there is only silence except for the persistent high pitched sound of tinitus ringing in my ears.

What are the good things about getting old? I did hear you right, didn't I? I've mentioned some of them. It's not really such a long list. Maybe we'll leave that for another day. I think I'll go and take a nap now.

TOO MUCH LOVE

"Then love me less, Pop," Jake had shouted.

"You mean...." his voice sputtered. "Is that really what you want - that I should love you less?"

There was silence on the other end of the phone.

"So! I shall try to love you less. To kill love needs some cooperation, but you're giving me plenty. All right, son, I shall try to love you not so much." His words were falling over one another, his tongue sticking to his palate in this language that he had learned as a young immigrant.

"Just remember," he added, pointing a finger at the phone as though it were at fault, "just remember if you change your mind - maybe you wouldn't like it so much - tell me. Just tell me."

"C'mon, Pop, you know what I mean. I'm not trying to hurt you - it's just that you shouldn't care so much ....it weighs on me - it puts pressure on me. Can't you...."

He was interrupted, "God forbid I should put pressure on you." His irony was not lost on his son.

"Pop, can't you try to understand? That's why we fight so much. Stop thinking I'm such a great guy and you won't be so disappointed in me. I'm just like anybody..."

"You want I should treat you just like anybody." It was a statement.

"Oh, Pop! You know what I mean. Just leave me be for a while. Stop caring so much about what I do and how I do it."

"I should stop caring." Again, it was a statement, not a question. "All right, I'll stop caring." His voice was defiant as he put the receiver down but his brown eyes, clouded by cataracts, glistened with tears. He got up painfully. How could he change himself now? Hadn't his own father cared too much - if that's what it was. His own father had pushed and argued and yes - loved - and helped him to grow up. Stop loving? He felt dizzy. He meant to put on his jacket and cap and go for a walk on this lovely spring day, but now his head was spinning and he sat down heavily on one of the old wooden carved dining chairs that had belonged to his parents before him.

The windows were open and a fresh breeze blew in carrying with it just a touch of winter. But the sun was shining and creating miniature points of light on the crystal decanter standing on the heavy sideboard. Birds were calling to one another in the trees which were just coming into bud. He longed for his wife. She had gone to visit their daughter and would be home later. She would scold him, he knew, for quarreling with their son in her absence, but her face would be filled with love for him and concern for them both. She wouldn't believe there could be too much love. She would never believe that.

The light-headedness passed and he put on his cap and scarf and walked outside. There is a special quality to the air in each season and in spring, the smell of the earth, the caress of the sparkling sunlit air sends lambs frolicking and children leaping for joy. He was old now, but he felt some of that antic energy seeping into his sluggish veins and osteoporotic bones. The breeze lightly stroked his parched wrinkled skin and the sun warmed his heart like a benediction. Had he been wrong, he wondered? Is it possible to love too much? Maybe what he thought was love wasn't love at all but a desperate wanting to hold on, to hold on to relevancy. He had once been a towering figure - all 5'7" of him - to his family. Now he was a side bar, an afterthought. All of a sudden - too quickly to allow for an adjustment - he had become a relic, a living memory, like a faded black and white photograph, to be put in an album and rarely looked at.

What is right? And who makes the rules anyway? You try to push your way back into the lives of your children and the more you push, the more strongly they push you out. "Would I have said such things to my father if he had lived as long as I have?" he asked himself, his lips moving in agitation. "I think not, but who knows what is what anymore? My boy is probably no better, no worse than any other."

Back at his front door he saw that his wife had returned. She was in the kitchen preparing some dinner and looking anxiously at the clock as he came in. She turned to him quizzically. She knew. She always knew even without asking when he was upset.

"So, Liebchen," he said, "how are Sarah and the baby? Oh, Jake called while you were out. He says I love him too much."

Printed in the United States
61687LVS00002B/61-108